January 30, 2025

A MENDING WOUND

Also by J. E. Ribbey

<u>The Last Patriots Series</u>

American post-apocalyptic thrillers

Fall of Freedom

Archangel

For You, My Dove

Rise of the Eagle

Operation Gray Owl

<u>Young American Adventures</u>

Middle grade historical fiction

The Innocent Rebel

Defiant Retreat

Under the Wing of the Storm

Deceptive Victory

A Mending Wound

A Mending
WOUND

by J. E. RIBBEY

Soraya Jubilee
PRESS

SORAYA JUBILEE PRESS
An imprint of The Jubilee Homestead LLC,
Stanchfield, Minnesota

SJ

Printed in the United States of America

LIBRARY OF CONGRESS CONTROL NUMBER: 2024921144

Print ISBN: 979-8-9899878-8-7
eBook ISBN: 979-8-9899878-9-4

Edited & cover design by Esther Ribbey

Cover image credit: The Battle of Stono Ferry, artist unknown

This is a work of fiction. Any similarity between the characters and
situations within its pages and places or persons, living or dead, is
unintentional and co-incidental.

To our own four young adventurers.

Chapter 1

April 17, 1779

This morning I awoke to the most beautiful chorus of birds singing outside the wagon. In my opinion, this is the surest sign the winter is over, and spring is finally here to stay. I was lost to the delightful melody, praising the Lord with all my soul, when Mrs. Bell called for me, her voice cutting through our praises like nails on slate. While I have come to admire her enthusiasm for righteous conduct, she seems nearly void of any humanity. The birds too, seemed to register the offense, and quit singing entirely, though for my part, I smiled to her sweetly as she threw open the canvas, destroying everything that was left of my peaceful morning.

This winter has been a winter of trials and growth. I reckon I now have the skin of a rhinoceros after enduring Mrs. Bell's omnipresent correction and

Mr. Musgrave's by-the-book management of our humble medical cabin. If Abigail were here, I'm sure I'd have worn her ears out with my complaining and tears, but she's not . . . Adelaide has even thicker skin than mine, on account she's had more practice, but even so, I've overheard her pouring out her frustrations when Ben is around.

Mr. Musgrave, for his part, means well. He has no confidence in our experience and must do everything according to the books. Unfortunately for our patients, we've learned a lot since his books were written and not all the written practices are sound. Adelaide and I do our best to accommodate his wishes, but our duty is to the patents, and there are times when we do not carry out his orders fully. I wish Captain Davis were here to correct him. For now, I patiently endure his reprimands for the sake of those under my care. Perhaps in time he will come to appreciate our collective wisdom in these matters, if only for the sake of the men.

Henry and I have grown ever more kindred in spirit over the long winter months as we are the only ones who can bear one another's loneliness. He longs for Abigail, Mary-Beth, David, and the tavern, but he will not rest until his beloved children can live out their lives in freedom. The long months away from his loved ones wearies his soul, we are all of us desperate to see the war's end. It saddens me to see so much of his playful nature sobered by the conflict.

Abe works tirelessly as a stableboy, keeping the army's horses fed and groomed, and their pens cleaned. Henry says he's treated well by the cavalry, and he chooses to sleep amongst them rather than come home to the wagon. I know he's just searching for himself in the middle of this tumultuous world, longing to prove he's a man when he's still just a fourteen-year-old boy. His heart has wandered, lost, since the day Papa took his stand on the green.

As for me, I miss my family wherever they may be. I miss the simplicity and slow pace of life before the war, and perhaps the little girl I was back then. And then, there is the part of me that misses Tobias, which is an altogether different kind of missing. I wait for his letters every day, even if I've just received one. I know it is folly to hope for a letter each day, but I anxiously await the post all the same. I always endeavor in my work to make him proud; I was foolish not to recognize how fortunate we were to have him. I worry for him; he's the kind to work himself to death if someone isn't there to tell him to rest.

I pray each day for victory and courage, for the wisdom of our leadership, and that the king and parliament would have mercy on the soldiers and their families on both sides and agree to allow us to govern ourselves. May God grant peace to those whose loved ones have paid the highest price. And may Providence shine upon our cause.

Mercy Young, 16 years old.

The ground squished under her feet as Mercy emerged from the wagon. The sun was rising on a crisp spring morning. Evening rains had soaked the ground that was beginning to green with fresh shoots of grass. Mrs. Bell and Adelaide were already up working the fire for breakfast, so she collected the pail and headed to the stream for water.

"I already fetched it while you were sleeping," Mrs. Bell said flatly.

"Yes, ma'am."

"If you didn't stay up to all hours scratching down all your feelings in that book, you'd be fit to rise with the rest of us."

Mercy cringed. "Yes, ma'am."

"She's only a half hour late, Mama," Jonathan said, dropping an armload of wood. "It isn't easy working with those who are sick and dying; writing helps her ease her mind."

Mrs. Bell pursed her lips.

She hadn't told him that—but he was right. And it wasn't the first time he'd come to her defense over the long winter.

"All the same, it's the Good Lord she should be taking a troubled mind to," Mrs. Bell finally replied.

"I do, ma'am," Mercy replied. "I write it all down."

Mrs. Bell sighed in defeat.

"I wouldn't mind a little water to freshen up," Jonathan piped up. "Splitting wood is a messy business."

"I'll go fetch some," Mercy said, taking up that pail once more.

"Can I come with?" Mable asked.

"Take a pail with you," Mrs. Bell said. "Lord knows we go through plenty of water."

Together the girls made their way to the stream. Mercy felt unsettled, it was awkward living with the Bells. Jonathan would never have defended Adelaide the way he'd just defended her. Mrs. Bell was clearly trying to mold her into her ideal woman, and Adelaide was already practically betrothed to her saintly older brother. All *she* wanted was a warm and dry place to sleep, and perhaps a little peace.

"He likes you," Mable said as they filled their pails. "Even though you gave him that embarrassing scolding last fall."

Mercy cringed for the second time that morning, lifting her pail from the water.

"Mama wants him to find a Puritan wife," Mable continued.

"Me too," Mercy agreed. "I think that would make everyone happy."

"Why aren't you a Puritan?" Mable asked.

Mercy thought for a moment. "Because I wasn't raised to be, I guess."

"But you could be one?"

"If I chose to be."

"Well, why not then?"

"I think that is a choice I'd have to think very hard about, and only commit to it if I truly believed that is what God wanted for me."

"Do you think we're wrong?" Mable asked.

"Not if that is what your faith says to do. The Bible says that man looks on the outward appearance, but God looks at the heart. What matters to Him is not what you're doing, but why you're doing it. If you're a Puritan because that's what your heart tells you is the best way to honor God, then be a Puritan. Right now, your family is Puritan, and the Bible tells us to honor our fathers and mothers, so for now, be the best one you can be until the Lord tells you differently."

"I'll be fifteen this year. In another year I'll be a woman, a short while after that I suppose I'll be married. That's our way, but I don't feel like I'm ready."

"I'm sure none of our mamas did either, but we turned out alright. Maybe it isn't so much about being ready, as it is having the faith to walk out whatever God gives us, knowing He's the one who's prepared us for it in the first place."

Mable smiled softly. "That's a more peaceful way of thinking about it."

Mercy ate her breakfast in silence. She didn't know where the words had come from, but they'd been a comfort to her as well. Perhaps it had been God Himself comforting them in the midst of their chaotic lives. She'd forgotten Mable was nearly fifteen, it was difficult to remember without the Bells celebrating birthdays. Where had the years gone?

After helping with the dishes, she and Adelaide tiptoed through the mud to the medical cabin. Inside they found Mr. Musgrave puffing on his pipe as he applied a damp rag to a fevered man's brow.

"We lost one during the night," he grumbled as they entered. "Fetch your aprons and let's see if we can bring these fevers down. Warmer days are nearly here, girls; we must hold out a bit longer."

"Yes, sir," Mercy said.

The winter had been mild compared to the last, and the added warmth and dryness of the cabins had aided them in keeping their casualties comparatively low. Still the pox and fever sent many a soldier to their graves, some even before they'd had the chance to face the enemy in the field.

"Still carry that owl about, miss?" her first patient asked.

"Yes," Mercy smiled. "Though Mr. Musgrave won't let me bring him in here."

"I remember him—" the man wheezed, "when we were bringing the guns up Dorchester Heights. You nearly worked yourself to death."

"We all did," Mercy said, dabbing his forehead.

"As soon as I'm back on my feet we'll whoop 'em again," the man coughed.

"That's right," Mercy said. "And you'd best be quick about it, the day is shaping up to be a warm one. It'll be time to fight again soon."

"I will, lass. I feel better already."

Mercy squeezed his hand gently before moving on to the next. Her next patient was sitting upright sipping a mug of coffee.

"You look much better today," Mercy said.

"Aye, I believe the fever broke last night. I slept like a baby," the man said with a smile.

Mercy felt his forehead with the back of her hand. "I believe you're right, though you may feel weak for a bit. It'd do you good to get back to your regiment, I'm sure they've been worried about you." She helped him up from the bed and he downed the rest of his coffee.

"Hopefully I won't see you for a bit," the man said. "Though it's been a pleasure to be under your care."

As he turned and started for the door, Mercy called after him. "Make sure you get something to eat."

"I will, miss."

"Another one back on the line," Musgrave said triumphantly, tapping out his pipe against his pegleg. "We're gaining the upper hand, praise God!"

Though there were dozens of other patients yet to rise from their beds, it felt good every time one did—a reward for their long and exhausting battle, victory over their invisible foe. Each time it gave them hope, a promise, that if they persisted, others would rise as well. And in that spirit Mercy moved on to the next, and the next, and the next. Always with a smile, always offering hope.

By day's end, her back was stiff and her feet sore, but she was making a difference, one life at a time. As she stepped out of the medical cabin, she took a deep breath of the cool fresh April air. Theo hopped down from under the eve where he'd been sleeping and landed gracefully on her shoulder. With spirits high, the two girls tiptoed their way back through the mud to the wagon feeling full.

Chapter 2

The weather continued to warm as April gave way to May. Rivers and streams once flooded by the spring melt were returning to their normal levels, which was just what Mercy needed to break up the monotony of camp life. Hidden amongst her things in the wagon was a tin of hooks—hidden because Mrs. Bell was willing to suffer firecakes to the end of the war if that's what it took to tame Mercy Young.

Her morning had gone smoothly, her patients were recovering well, bandages were washed and dried, notes scribbled in her journal, and now it was time. The tricky part was that Mrs. Bell was at the wagon teaching school to the camp children. Mercy kicked herself for not grabbing the hooks and thread that morning before they'd left, but she'd been too busy worrying about her posture while she ate breakfast to think about much else.

Arriving at the wagon, the girls split up; Adelaide headed to the buckboard as a distraction while Mercy headed for the back.

"Hi, Mama," Adelaide said.

"You girls finished for the morning?" Mrs. Bell asked.

Mercy crept quietly to the back of the wagon and pulled herself up.

"Yes, we just finished," Adelaide said.

"Hmmm," Mrs. Bell replied. "And where is Mercy?"

Mercy froze; Adelaide wouldn't lie, especially to her mother.

"She's . . . around."

Mercy reached gingerly for the little box that held her diary, inkwell, thread, a half-dozen corks she'd been collecting, and the hooks. Lifting it gingerly from its place, her foot slipped off the wagon wheel, dumping her into the wagon and sending Theo flopping and fluttering through the handful of surprised children before bouncing off Mrs. Bell on his way out of the front of the wagon.

"Good heavens, Mercy Young!" Mrs. Bell exclaimed. "Are you destined to bring chaos and disorder wherever you go?!"

Mercy peeled herself out of a pile of blankets as a half-dozen wide-eyed children grinned knowingly about the berating they were about to witness.

"Sorry, ma'am," Mercy said, pulling her dangling legs into the wagon. "I was just trying to fetch my box without disturbing you."

"Well, consider me disturbed! A *lady* would ask respectfully to interrupt momentarily to collect her things."

"Yes, ma'am," Mercy replied, hanging her head.

"Now, fetch your box and go. And as you go, let your soul reflect on your character and how you could do better in the future."

"Yes, ma'am," Mercy said, taking the box and climbing out of the back of the wagon. Her ribs ached from where the back board had cut into them when her legs had kicked out, but her pride hurt too. She didn't try to fail Mrs. Bell, but she just wasn't any good at being Mrs. Bell.

She met Adelaide at the front of the wagon and the two of them set off. Mrs. Bell still appeared too flustered to even wonder about where they were going.

Once they were a safe distance away, Adelaide said, "Well, that's one way to get them."

"Easy for you to say, she didn't make you out to be a daft idiot in front of the whole camp," Mercy grumbled.

"The camp knows you, Mercy. To the children you're a hero—Theo too. That's probably the most they've smiled all day."

"I don't want to be the camp jester," Mercy said. "I just want to be . . . me."

"Everyone makes mistakes, Mercy. No one could be as courageous and adventurous as you and not make mistakes, those who don't, have never tried. Only someone who's doing something could have a slip while doing it. That's why it's always the doers who are the most criticized, because those who aren't doing don't have anything to be criticized about."

"It's my 'doin'' that's got your mama so flustered," Mercy retorted.

"You're just different, Mercy. She doesn't understand you, but she means well. She *does* cherish you, that's why she's taking such a keen interest on making you into a respectable woman."

"Sometimes her *cherishing* is smothering."

"And some of it has been good for you," Adelaide added. "Everyone God puts in our lives is to help shape us in one way or another . . . you just have to have faith. The Good Lord knows what He's doing. I know you've helped shape *my* life." She smiled.

Mercy smiled back. "And you've shaped mine."

The girls made their way to the stream and snapped off two saplings to serve as canes. Mercy tied on the thread and added hooks. Icy water tumbled and boiled over submerged boulders as it continued on its endless journey to the sea. Flipping a couple of large rocks produced a handful of worms and the girls were set.

"What's your mama going to think when we come back with fish?" Mercy asked. "She's already in a dither."

"Mama loves eating fish, don't fret, her stomach will win out. She'll chide us out of duty, but inwardly she'll be grateful. Why do you think she didn't ask us where we were going?"

Mercy looked at her.

"Because she already knew what we were up to." Adelaide smiled.

Mercy smiled back with a sigh. "We've got good mamas, don't we?"

Adelaide nodded.

Presently Adelaide's cork swirled around a boulder before plunging beneath the surface. Setting the hook, her sapling nearly doubled over as she battled a heavy trout in the churning current. Mercy brought her line in and slipped out of her shoes and stockings. Wading into the frigid water, she helped Adelaide land the fish.

"That's a good one!" Mercy said admiringly.

"Mama will be happy." Adelaide smiled.

"A fish like that makes the berating worthwhile," Mercy agreed.

Climbing ashore, Mercy slipped the fish onto a willow branch and swung her line back out into the water. As she watched her cork bob in the current, she pondered what Adelaide had said. People were complicated. There was their exterior—the way they behaved, often based on others' expectations, or principles of society. Then there was an inner person—who may not agree entirely with the person they were on the outside. Perhaps that is what the Bible was talking about when it said that man looks on the outward appearance, but God looks at the heart.

We can look a certain way on the outside, follow the rules, be courteous, maybe even smile while we do, but if that isn't the spirit of the inner person, then in God's eyes, it's all for naught. She felt that God would not want there to be a difference between the two; that to be genuine, she should be the same person on the outside as she was on the inside, and if one needed work, they both did. It wasn't easy; it's *much* easier to put on the person everyone wants to see for a moment, than to truly change one's character.

Her thoughts were forced to wait as her cork disappeared from the surface; she set the hook hard, and to Theo's delight, a small fish came blasting from the surface, spraying water onto her dress. The fish flew over her head and landed amongst the dead leaf litter behind her.

"Goodness, Mercy," Adelaide laughed. "For a moment that fish thought it was a bird!"

"I had visions of one like yours," Mercy laughed at herself. "Here you go, Theo," she said, unhooking the little trout. "First one of the season." Rebaiting her hook, she swung her line back out into the water.

"Have you heard from the captain recently?" Adelaide asked.

"His letters are often delayed or not delivered at all on account they may fall into enemy hands and reveal something of strategic importance inadvertently."

"He's a fine prospect." Adelaide smiled.

"Prospect?!" Mercy gasped. "No . . . we're just dear friends."

"Uh huh."

"Neither of us could even imagine getting romantically involved with anyone at a time like this, it just isn't prudent."

Adelaide looked at her a little wounded.

"Imprudent for people like us, that is," Mercy clarified. "You and Ben are a different sort, stronger, able to bear the heartache. Worry like that would be the death of me."

"Ah." Adelaide nodded sarcastically.

Mercy looked at her toes, willing another fish to bite and break up the awkwardness. And in the moment, she felt a slight ache, deep inside.

"But I do miss him," Mercy admitted.

"I know," Adelaide replied, staring out into the stream.

A few minutes of silence passed between them before Adelaide's cork disappeared once more and a plump trout was able to pull them from their longings. Mercy plucked the fish from the stream and slid it onto the willow branch.

Four more trout were added, and it was time to return to camp. Their lines were wrapped around the saplings and the hook buried in the bark until next time. Mercy carried the willow branch of fish while Adelaide carried the rods.

When they came in sight of the wagon, Mrs. Bell rose from her seat near the fire with her hands on her hips.

"Oh boy . . ." Mercy mumbled.

"Just look at you two fine ladies," Mrs. Bell said sarcastically. "Enjoyed a little romp in the woods, did we?"

"We caught some fish for dinner, Mama," Adelaide said.

"I can see that," Mrs. Bell said.

"Jesus seemed to favor fishermen," Mercy said. "And He always seems fit to bless our endeavors, ma'am."

Mrs. Bell stared at them, at a loss for what to say. Mercy had figured out early on that it was best to bring the Lord into it and let Him do her fighting for her. Mrs. Bell would never dare cross the Lord.

"Well, since it is the Lord's bounty . . ." Mrs. Bell said at last.

"I'll clean 'em for you, Mama," Jonathan said, having just returned from his sentry duty.

Mercy handed him the fish with a subtle curtsy.

"It'll be a blessing to have something fresh to eat for a change," Jonathan said, smiling gratefully.

Mercy watched him turn and start for the wagon.

"Well, don't just stand there, girls," Mrs. Bell said. "Mercy, go fetch some water; Adelaide, bring the pan and some lard; Mable, fetch the salt."

Theo ruffled his feathers as Mercy reached for the pail. "I know, boy, she could have said please . . ."

Mercy stopped at the stream, setting her pail down for a moment to take in the afternoon beauty. Sunlight shimmered on the rippling current, young leaves created a green haze in the forest around her, and white blossoms adorned the wild plumb bushes. Birds chased one another in the young spruce near the water's edge, singing loudly as they flitted about the boughs.

Theo stretched his wings on her shoulder before resettling his feet and the merriment amongst the spruces froze, the singing stopped, everything was still except the churning river. Mercy squinted into the boughs across the stream, but her eyes couldn't make out a one of the dozen or so little birds who'd been there only a moment ago. It was incredible, like they'd just vanished.

Footfalls behind her sent her into a panic and she plunged her pail into the water and withdrew it, turning to start back.

"Woah!" Jonathan said as she nearly bumped right into him, her pail splashing water onto his breeches. "Sorry, I didn't mean to startle you."

Mercy gasped, holding her hand on her chest.

"I finished cleaning the fish and needed to clean my knife and hands. You'd hadn't come back yet so I thought I'd just wash them here."

"I was on my way," Mercy said swiftly.

"I can see that. Is everything alright? You've been gone—"

"I'm fine, just got lost in my thoughts," she said, moving to step around him.

"If you wait a minute, I'll walk you back."

Mercy cringed, but she'd made Adelaide a promise to treat him fairly. "Alright."

Jonathan rinsed his hands and knife in the stream under Theo's watchful gaze. Standing, he slid the knife back into its leather sheath and slid the sheath into his waistband before drying his hands on his breeches.

"I don't think your owl likes me," he said, taking note of Theo's careful tracking.

"He doesn't trust you," Mercy replied. "But he didn't trust Captain Davis for a couple of years, so you needn't worry."

"It's peculiar, the way he watches over you."

"It's a blessing, I've got no one else." As soon as she'd said it, she wished she could take it back.

He looked at her, his eyes probing her own, a soft smile lifting the corners of his mouth. After a moment, he shifted his gaze past her. "Well, we'd best get back before Mama comes looking for you."

Mercy nodded and together they started back up the path towards the wagon.

Chapter 3

"Blast these red vultures!" Flint Musgrave ranted as he returned from a meeting.

"What is it?" Mercy asked, helping him out of his dress coat.

"They've been raiding us north and south, up and down the Chesapeake, and they hit Charlestown[1] too! Burning, looting, and running off before anyone can catch 'em!"

"But how?" Mercy asked.

"Their navy. They show up without warning and rush ashore; there's nothing our folks can do about it! Some ally the French turned out to be . . ." he fumed. "They struck first on the tenth of May and here it's the 23rd and they're still at it, and we've no navy to stop 'em."

"Has anyone been hurt?" Adelaide asked.

---

[1] Present-time Charleston

"The militias are no match for them, not on such short notice; they run when they first set eyes on the lobsterbacks."

"What are they burning?" Mercy asked.

"Merchant ships, cotton, tobacco, hay and fodder, anything they can't carry. That General Clinton is trying to draw us out into a battle of his choosing, even if he has to starve us into fighting. Folks are angry—angry at the redcoats for what they've been doing, angry at us for not stopping them."

"I can understand that," Mercy said. "It'd be difficult to feel anything but anger watching your livelihood burn to the ground."

"If only we had a navy," Flint grumbled as he sat messaging his stump.

"It seems like the war will go on forever if we just continue to sit and wait," Mercy said.

"Aye, but if we rush in, it may be over quickly and not in our favor. Don't be fooled by their apparent successes, lass. They're as desperate as we are. I've heard word this war is bankrupting the king."

"Then why doesn't he just quit?" Adelaide asked.

"Because," Musgrave grunted as he lifted himself from his chair. "If they lose, they'll have to pay for the war."

"And if we lose, we will?" Mercy asked.

"That's right. He'll tax us for it."

"It's always about money," Adelaide said.

"I suppose all wars are. What's the point if not to increase the wealth and power of your nation? Whether the Romans, Greeks, Persians, Egyptians, British, Spanish, or French, it's always been about increasing the wealth, might, and influence of the kingdom."

"And all the widows and orphans, and suffering?" Mercy asked.

"The cost of achieving that wealth."

"Will we be different?" asked Mercy.

"I don't know," Flint said, scratching his grizzly chin. "I think we'd like to be, but men with power seem often tempted to abuse it. Only by God's grace and leading could we truly endeavor to create a government that would be by the people and for the people."

"I pray for these boys' sakes it is so," Mercy sighed.

Later that evening, Henry, Ben, and Abe joined Mercy and the Bells for supper. It wasn't unusual for them to spend the evenings together, but Ben's nervous excitement conveyed there was more going on than just having a family meal.

"How are we this evening, Mrs. Bell?" Henry said as they sat.

"As well as one bereft of her husband, her home, and her comforts, called to toil in the mire by God's good grace can be, I expect."

"Uhhh, that's good . . ." Henry said.

"Mercy! If you don't get that blasted creature to step back from the pot while I'm cooking, it'll be him were eating, so help me!" Mrs. Bell said, wiping her forehead with the back of her hand.

Mercy jumped up and snatched Theo from the pole holding the pot over the fire, placing him on the buckboard.

Mrs. Bell and Adelaide dished up the stew until everyone had a bowl. Jonathan said grace, and everyone began eating. Mercy watched Ben curiously as he fidgeted with his bowl but seemed too nervous to eat. Mercy was nearly done with her stew by the time he got up the courage and cleared his throat.

"Mrs. Bell, Jonathan," he began. "We've been given some leave, and I was wondering if I might, with your permission, take Adelaide with Henry, Abe, and myself to look in on our farm in Lexington."

Mercy's brow furrowed. *Why would he want Adelaide to go and not herself?*

"Why would Adelaide be interested in that?" Mrs. Bell asked.

Mercy looked over at Adelaide who seemed just as curious to know the answer.

"Well, ma'am," Henry cut in. "In the absence of his father, the farm rightly falls to him."

"What are you saying?!" Mercy blurted. "Papa's going to come back . . ."

"It's been four years, Mercy," Henry said softly. "I've sent dozens of letters of inquiry; I've never received a one in return."

Mercy stared at the two of them in shocked disbelief.

"Mercy," Henry said. "I know this is difficult to hear, but prison conditions do not allow for long life. Ben and I mean no disrespect to your papa, quite the opposite, you and I both know your papa would want him to have it. He would be proud to see his son carry on the farm in his stead."

She didn't know what to think. What were they saying? That he was dead? That all their fighting, all her writing and waiting was for nothing?

Tears filled her eyes, and before she could think, she jumped from her stump and ran into the safety of the woods and darkness beyond the firelight.

It wasn't that she'd failed to recognize her father's death as a possibility—she had—only in her mind it had always been an impossible possibility. So long as it was impossible, she didn't have to face it, she could keep on writing, keep on hoping, keep on believing that one day he'd come home and be proud of the woman she'd become.

She stopped running. Heaving in deep painful gasps, she let the tears fall. She couldn't lose him too…

She imagined him, dying, cold and alone in some damp prison cell, or perhaps he'd not even survived the trip across the sea. His body cast into the ocean without so much as a hymn or a prayer.

"Why?" she asked, looking to the sky. "Why have you taken them from me?"

"Mercy?!" a voice called.

"He-he-here," she answered, trying to control her sobs.

In a moment, Ben stepped up beside her and wrapped her in his arms.

Burying her face in his neck, she sobbed.

"I know," Ben choked. "I can't imagine him being gone either."

"Why?" Mercy sobbed.

"I don't know, Mercy. I don't know. When Henry first brought up the idea about the farm, I didn't want to face it either. But our foraging patrols are long, and a fella has a lot of time to think. Papa wouldn't want the farm to decay, or to go to someone else . . . it's our farm, the Young farm. I knew Henry was right, even though it pained me to hear it, Papa and Mama built that farm for us."

"I kn-know . . ." Mercy sniffled. "But why?"

"The way I see it, taking the farm is a way of keeping him and Mama alive. We're their legacy, we *are* the Youngs now."

She knew he was right. Papa would be proud to have him inherit the farm. But not now, years from now, when he was old and grey, and had watched his grandchildren play on the green.

"They wouldn't want you to stay sad either, Mercy. Papa went out on that green to give us a chance at a life he never had. If he could see us now, I think he'd be proud."

"I know," Mercy said. "I just don't know where he is . . . how—how can I say goodbye if I don't know where he is?"

Ben pulled her in even tighter. "I know . . . it isn't fair, Mercy. The Lord will tell him, the Good Lord will tell him for you."

She couldn't hold it back any longer, and she went limp in his arms, sobbing in agony. Ben held her, assuring her that it was okay, she could break, and he would hold her.

He stayed with her as the time passed irreverently, holding on as her papa was torn from her. It was a pain like none other she'd ever endured, and, in that moment, she wondered if she would. It was as if the north star had fallen from the sky, and she found herself adrift in a tumultuous sea without a way to find her bearings.

But then she felt something, something strange. In the midst of all her grief she felt a peace. The Lord wouldn't have abandoned their papa, and he couldn't have died alone if the Lord was with him. And that same Lord hadn't abandoned them either, He'd always made a way, brought them here, and their papa would want them to continue.

"You could come back with us . . ." Ben said as her sobs subsided.

She thought about it for a moment. "No, take Adelaide. I think I need some time to let him go and mourn; I'm afraid I'd see him everywhere and your trip would be an abysmal one."

"That's if Mrs. Bell and Jonathan give me their blessing," he said. "I came after you before I heard their reply."

"Then you've got to go back," Mercy said, pushing them apart. "It's your farm now, both of yours."

"Alright," he smiled. "But don't you stay out here for too long."

"I'll be along."

She listened to his footfalls fade into the dark. She'd lost a lot, but she hadn't lost everyone. She looked to the sky as tears filled her eyes once more and thanked the Lord for the ones she had left, and for the good ones she'd had, that one day she'd see again.

Life was so tragic—and beautiful, and painful, and lovely, and empty, and full. And somehow, she was supposed to play her part in it, by faith, never knowing what lovely or terrible thing may lay just ahead. Trusting the Good Shepherd with her days whether they be long or short, that it all, in the end, is worthwhile.

Swirling amongst her sorrows was a glimmer of joy. Ben would be taking his future bride to see their home. An empty home that would once again be filled with life, joy and sorrow, toil and rest. And the warmth of the thought comforted her as her heart longed for Papa.

She lingered, wrapped in the cool night's embrace until she knew she'd cause the others to worry if she didn't return. It would take time for the wound to heal and become a scar like the passing of her mother. They were truly orphans now . . .

Emerging from the dark, she saw Adelaide sitting beside Ben unaware of her adoring smile as she listened to him describe the family farm. Jonathan caught sight of her and stood from his seat, and everyone stopped talking.

"I'm sorry for running off," Mercy said awkwardly.

"Don't be," Jonathan answered for everyone. "I know what it's like . . . I'm truly sorry, Mercy."

Mercy nodded, taking her seat on the stump. "So, are you going to Lexington?" she asked Adelaide.

"Yes." Adelaide smiled. "We'll be leaving in the morning, though I wish you were joining us."

"Next time," Mercy said. "Flint needs someone who knows how to care for folks."

"That's true," Adelaide agreed. "Will you be alright?"

"I'm okay," Mercy said. "Just have to go through it."

Henry rolled his barrel beside her stump and sat down. He didn't say a word, he simply wrapped his arm around her and pulled her in close as the conversations resumed around the fire.

Mercy's breath caught in her throat as she leaned over and laid her head on his shoulder.

"Please . . . don't leave me," she whispered.

His embrace tightened and he laid his head against hers. "Never," he whispered.

That night when Mercy returned to the wagon, she opened her diary. Dipping the quill into the inkwell, she trembled as she brought it to the page. She'd write about him, the man who'd raised them, cared for them, and protected them. A good man, a father, and a friend, who'd always believed in her. She'd write, through the pain and loneliness, so that his life would not be forgotten.

Slowly the quill began scratching parchment, immortalizing his story. For the first time she wasn't writing to him, but to those who'd come after, so that they'd know the man who'd taken a stand so they could be free. A single spark, a life sowed in hope.

And she knew they had to win. Her papa's legacy wasn't a simple farm in a simple town. His legacy was freedom. The first among courageous men who'd looked the king's soldiers in the eye and said, "no more," his defiance echoing still in their banner flapping proudly in an American breeze.

That was her papa.

She wrote until the tears blurred her vision, wiped them away, and wrote some more. Line by line she felt her heart lighten as she remembered the man she'd been proud to call papa. And she prayed, that if by some miracle he was still out there somewhere, that the Good Lord would let him know her feelings this night.

When at last she finished, and her eyes were all cried out, she blew out her candle and went to sleep proud that she'd been born a Young.

Chapter 4

The days without Henry, Benjamin, or Adelaide were the loneliest. Her morning had passed uneventfully with the exception of tending to a soldier who'd received lashings for being drunk on duty. Flint had regaled her with tales of times even General Benidict Arnold had been drunk on duty, but it had never seemed to affect his soldiering other than make him a little surly. Even when he'd been wounded at Saratoga the general had gone deep into his cups before returning gallantly to the fight.

Mercy had never witnessed a time when drunkenness brought out the better in a man's character and appreciated the fact that the men in her life only drank ale or cider in moderation. Though she knew there were boys and men who couldn't seem to find relief from the horrors of the battlefield apart from ale, for them the cure was hardly better than the sickness. A pitiful plight to befall good men whose hearts could bear no more.

She'd finished her duties and returned to the wagon, preparing to set out with Theo in search of fish. Collecting one of the canes, they made for the path that led to the stream. The days were growing steadily warmer, and she paused her thoughts to thank God for the thick leaves overhead shielding her from the sun's rays.

Arriving at the stream, she took a seat on a boulder and breathed in the beauty and simplicity of it. The stream, clear and cool, rolled over the rocks, glimmering in dazzling display. Theo nudged her gently, looking expectantly into her eyes.

"Alright," she sighed. "I don't know what your hurry is, we have all afternoon."

Turning over a couple of smaller rocks, she found a plump worm. She slipped it onto her hook and flicked the line out into the current. Leaning back, she closed her eyes, content to wait until a fish found her bait.

It had been a few days since she'd been forced to accept that her papa was probably amongst the casualties of the war for freedom. Though it still ached to think about, the shock had lost its sting, replaced by a sad emptiness where hope had once burned so brightly. Still, she saw the Lord's merciful hand in guiding their lives, and her papa could rest in peace knowing they were well cared for.

"It isn't safe for a lady to be out here alone."

Mercy sat up, squinting in the bright sunlight. As her eyes adjusted, she recognized Jonathan.

"I'm not alone," she replied. "I have Theo."

"Still, there are savages, Tories, bears, and mountain lions; if something happened, no one would find you out here."

Mercy didn't reply.

"Having any luck?" he asked, taking a seat on a boulder to her left.

"No," she replied. "Sometimes it takes a while."

"Well, I have every confidence you'll succeed," he said.

"I thought you were of the opinion that women shouldn't participate in these sorts of activities?"

He overturned a stone with the toe of his shoe. "After some further reflection, I have concluded that there is nothing in the Good Book that says a woman can't fish or hunt, and if God hasn't seen fit to command one way or the other, perhaps I shouldn't either."

"Sounds like wisdom," Mercy replied.

The cane jerked in her hand, and she set the hook. A brown stripped fish nearly ripped her rod from her hand as it darted for deeper water.

Her sapling doubled over as the fish fought to reach the security of a deadfall. Mercy followed the fish, tracking it along the shore, willing her line to hold. The fish turned and leapt from the water, shaking furiously before darting once more for the deadfall upon its return.

"It's going to break," Mercy squealed.

"Give it here," Jonathan said, taking the rod and stepping into the river.

He was knee deep by the time the fish wore itself out. Sloshing his way to shore, he dragged the fish out of the water.

"That was an adventure," he said, handing the rod back to her.

"Thank you," she replied. "It's a right good fish."

"Aye, a couple more like that and we'll have dinner."

He pruned a thin branch off a nearby tree and removed the twigs with his knife. Mercy took the branch and slid the fish onto it.

"Would you like to take a turn?" Mercy asked.

"Sure."

"We'll have to find another worm."

In a few minutes, the line was back in the water.

"You know . . . my father had a shop in Boston, like your farm in Lexington."

"What kind of shop?" Mercy asked.

"Shoes, he made shoes. And my mama sewed dresses— Puritan dresses that is."

"That's a good trade," Mercy replied. "Everyone needs shoes."

"It is, I used to help him. I miss him every day."

Mercy looked over at him. His eyes were lost, staring into the stream. "When the war is over, will you make shoes?" she asked.

"I don't know," he said. "It's the only thing I know how to do, but I like the adventure of being in the wild. I've pondered what it would be like to be a pioneer and set out into the unknown lands to the west. But that's just a silly dream. I have Mama, Mable, and Nathaniel to look after."

"I don't think it's silly," Mercy said. "Mable is growing up fast, and your mama is very capable. Many a good man in the Bible spent time in the wilderness and came out the better for it."

"So, you think I need time in the wilderness, 'eh?"

"Couldn't hurt," Mercy smirked.

Jonathan snorted and shook his head.

The rod jerked and Jonathan set the hook, pulling the line from the water—empty. He held up the bare hook for her to see with a frown.

"Don't worry. Happens to me all the time," Mercy said. Flipping over a couple of rocks, she found another worm. "Swing it here and I'll put it on," Mercy said.

He studied her as she threaded the worm onto the hook with muddy fingers. "You *are* different, Mercy Young."

"Sorry," she said, letting the line go free as she finished.

"Don't be," he said, swinging it out into the current.

Stepping closer to the water, she squatted down and washed her hands. Maybe Abigail had been right, maybe she'd been wrong about him. He was clumsy in conversation, but sincere, and she *did* feel safer with him there. Standing from the water, she took a seat on her boulder.

"You know, when I was a boy, I couldn't wait to be a man," he said, looking out into the stream. "I thought my pa knew everything; he was wise, always had an answer to every question, and I thought when I was a man like him, I'd have all the answers too."

She watched him as he pondered his thoughts.

"But it isn't like that," he said, looking at her. "I don't have any answers . . . and I don't have my pa." He tossed a pebble into the stream.

"My papa was like that too," Mercy said.

"They make it look so easy," Jonathan said.

"Maybe it wasn't always about making the right decisions or having the right answer but doing right by the decisions they made. As far as we're able, we're to choose what is best, but I think it's more important how we fulfill those choices. My papa wanted us to live free, he showed us the integrity of his character when he marched out on the green . . . It was the last time we ever saw him. Most folks looking at the outcome would say that was a bad decision, but his character in that decision is what has led us here, and that's an incredible thing."

"That's one thing our fathers had in common; they walked out their convictions, whatever the cost."

"Maybe that's all you need to do," Mercy said.

He smiled over at her, tossing another pebble into the water. "I misjudged you—the day I told you it'd be better if you stayed silent."

"Yes, you did." Mercy smirked.

Jonathan snorted. "And . . ."

"And what?"

"Did you—possibly—misjudge me?" he asked.

"I don't know," Mercy frowned thoughtfully. "Time will tell."

He stared at her in disbelief.

"Looks like you're getting a nibble," she said, gesturing to the cane.

As he set the hook, she smiled; once again, she'd taken the high ground.

A few days later Henry, the boys, and Adelaide returned from Lexington. Joy mixed with sorrow as she remembered why they'd gone. It was good to have her friend back again and she couldn't wait to hear all about their trip while they worked together tending to patients. Benjamin and Henry seemed confident that with a little work, the farm could be restored to what it had been.

A neighbor, seeing the fields empty, had continued to farm them as his own, but promised to return them to Ben when he was ready. The house had suffered some decay, and Henry had taught Ben how to patch the roof while they'd stayed there. It would take work, but Ben didn't seem to mind. The notion that he had a place only amplified his affections for Adelaide.

Mercy prayed, asking the Lord to see them through the war. Love as precious as theirs deserved a chance to grow.

The following day as they were completing their rounds, Adelaide brought a basket of bandages out to Mercy at the cauldron.

"So?" Mercy asked.

"So what?" Adelaide replied with a knowing smile.

"How did it go?" Mercy asked, pretending to swat her friend with the paddle.

"Long." Adelaide frowned. "And bumpy."

This time Mercy did swat her with the paddle. "I know what the trip is like!" Mercy growled playfully.

"Okay, okay!" Adelaide squealed, rubbing her bottom. "I'll tell you."

"Good!" Mercy said, pulling her down to sit beside her.

"I like it," Adelaide began. "The town is quaint compared to Boston, peaceful. Folks were excited to see Ben all grown up, and many of them gave their condolences concerning your papa, I can tell he was respected by everyone."

"He was," Mercy agreed.

"The land is beginning to sprout corn in long rows. A neighbor, Saul Graham, is farming it, but he said as soon as Ben is ready, he'll return the land. Henry said it's good that it's being worked in your family's absence."

"In *your* family's absence," Mercy said, squeezing Adelaide's hand.

To her surprise, Adelaide closed her eyes as a solitary tear rolled down her cheek.

"What is it?" Mercy asked in alarm.

"It seems so close now," Adelaide said. "I'm afraid now more than ever to hope for it."

Mercy put her arm around her and pulled her to her side, resting Adelaide's head on her shoulder.

"I walked through the house . . . *my* house," she whispered. "I touched my stove and drank water from our well. I sat in our room. I could see it, Mercy. I could see all of it, our family. Farming, and working, and loving, and playing . . . And I'm so afraid. What if he goes out there and doesn't come back? What if it all becomes just a dream?"

"He'll come back," Mercy said.

"Like your papa? Like mine?" Adelaide convulsed.

Mercy didn't know what to say. The war didn't differentiate between young and old, or those in love and those who loved nothing. It was an unbiased cruelty, and her friend knew it as well as anyone. It was unfair—that days that should be filled with such joy and anticipation were robbed by fear and dread.

"If it wasn't for our papas, you and Ben wouldn't have come together," Mercy said. "I don't think they, or the Lord for that matter, would want you to spoil the life they hoped to give you with thoughts of losing it. We don't get to decide when our time is done, and that ought to make us take joy in the time we do have all the more. What you have with Ben *is* real, right now, and what will be, will be. Fretting won't protect him; it'll only steal the time you have now."

Adelaide nodded, though her tears continued to fall.

"I do love him, Mercy."

"I know," Mercy said.

Chapter 5

June 24, 1779

My Dear Friend,

The post has been so unpredictable these past months that I've found myself in a state of hopelessness concerning our correspondence. It was with great joy that three of your letters were delivered to me, albeit previously read by the censor. I am delighted to hear the better lodgings and supply had a dramatic effect on the fever this past winter, and that Mr. Musgrave is beginning to acknowledge your experience.

I found myself grinning with joy upon hearing the progress of my friends Benjamin and Adelaide as they move ever closer to union. It is good that war is unable to stop the forces of love, no matter how dark the days we endure. They are as right and humble a couple as I have seen in all the states, and I am sure by God's good providence, they shall be among the first to wed in our free country.

Know that I grieve with you as you mourn the likely loss of your father. One of my regrets is never having the opportunity to know such a man, though I am deeply honored to call his daughter my dearest friend. This war has put the cost of freedom into vivid perspective, it isn't a wonder it is such a rare thing on the earth. He is among the lucky few to have been there that day as the first to take a stand and make his conscience heard. They will surely all go down in the history books as heroes to whom this nation owes its conception.

The war here in the South is a bitter and desperate struggle. Over the past weeks we've endured an army of redcoats, employed by General Lord Cornwallis, to pillage the countryside around Charlestown, aiming to capture the city itself. General Benjamin Lincoln was dispatched to provide relief for our militia there and met the enemy on the twentieth.

Our army, being much the younger, and mostly militia, was able to repel the invaders after a desperate battle at Stono Ferry. We took tragic losses, and our undisciplined troops scattered during the fight. We lost more than thirty who were killed, and five times that wounded, but most unsettling have been the desertions. There are more than one hundred and fifty militia still unaccounted for. If only we'd had the foresight to prepare our armies in the South.

My aid tents are bursting with casualties, and I find myself working day and night. Many times, in my fatigue I've thought I caught a glimpse of you moving amongst the cots, and my heart begins to stir, but upon further inspection it is one of my southern aides. I've never experienced an emptiness like this before, and I cannot rationalize it away. It seems to be beyond my understanding or control, and I cannot find a way to satisfy it.

Your letters offer temporary relief but leave me longing all the more to return to you all. I'd give my right arm for just one swift jesting retort at my expense. Your manner of correction, both amusing and accurate, make up many of my fondest memories. And if I'm being honest, a certain incident involving a water pail also brings a smile to my face.

Thank you for laboring in your letters on my behalf. They are a ray of sunshine, and the comfort of a friend. Let us continue to resolve to give our lives for the cause, that we may be found worthy to live in its victory.

Your friend,

Tobias Davis

Mercy folded up the letter and placed it in her apron. It was the first she'd received in over a month, and she found herself both relieved at its arrival and sad it ended so soon. There was no telling when the next letter would arrive or what events may take place before she received it. She'd thought she'd grown accustomed to his absence, but the longing that rose in her confirmed she'd only buried it in business.

"Why the long face?" Henry asked, puffing on his pipe. "Is the captain not faring well?"

Mercy had joined him on sentry duty that evening as it gave them time to be together and she much preferred it to Mrs. Bell's tedious correction of her posture.

"He's fine," Mercy mumbled. "Though it sounds as though they are making little headway."

"Then what is it?"

"I don't know . . . our correspondence is bitterly slow, and his letters end all too quickly. No sooner have I begun to rejoice at receiving his post then it's over, and I'm left . . . unsatisfied."

"I agree," Henry said, taking a puff. "The post makes a poor substitute for a person."

"It seems ungrateful," Mercy said. "I'm surrounded by fine folks, people I love, and yet, there's a part of me that still feels alone."

"I think that's only natural. We become a part of one another, love does that, and when we're apart, it only makes sense there would be an emptiness. I feel it too, Abigail, David, Mary-Beth . . . I long for them all."

"Me too . . ." Mercy sighed.

"I hear you and Jonathan Bell have been talking," Henry said. "A year ago, I wouldn't have thought that possible."

"He's come to find he misjudged me," Mercy said. "Told me as much."

"Ahh, and you've chosen to forgive him?"

"I'm not vengeful, Papa. I can sense his sincerity."

"Does that mean you misjudged him as well?"

"Perhaps, but I won't be saying as much. If I've learned anything growing up amongst boys, it's to maintain every advantage, there's no telling when they'll have the next foolish notion."

"Foolish like . . . the possibility of you being wrong?"

"Precisely," Mercy smirked. "The Bible tells us to be shrewd as serpents."

"And innocent as doves . . ." Henry added.

"I'll admit I'm wrong when the opportunity arises that it serves the occasion."

"We *are* talking about relationships, right? Not the battlefield?" Henry asked.

"Yes, but in my experience there's hardly a difference," Mercy said plainly.

"I can understand that, growing up with your brothers, but I feel . . . perhaps your relationship tactics could stand a little maturing, now that your relationships are changing," Henry posed tactfully.

"How so?" Mercy asked.

"Well," Henry said, running his hand through his hair. "I've always found it best in these sorts of relationships to be humble and forthcoming, right or wrong. Humble honesty being the best way to nurture a healthy, mutually respectful, and meaningful relationship of this nature."

"Of what nature?" Mercy asked.

"You know . . ." he said, combing his hand through his hair again. "A young man pursuing a young lady."

"I thought the point of being pursued was to make them catch you?" Mercy asked.

"It is, it is," Henry replied. "But the purpose of the pursuit is so you can see the depth and length of their character, not to give yourself the pleasure of humiliating the pursuers."

"I know," Mercy sighed. "Mama said to take things slow and let God work it out. The truth is, I'm not even sure I want to be pursued. Most days it's all I can do just to survive the day . . . I'm not ready for all that other stuff. I'm excited for Adelaide and Ben, but that's just not me. Not yet anyway."

Henry smiled.

"What?" Mercy asked.

"It gives me some relief to hear you say that. I'm afraid my heart is not ready to let you go just yet."

"No one told me growing up would be so complicated."

"This point is especially so," Henry agreed. "You are at the point in your road where there are many forks, each one leading to a different life, and you can only see their beginnings, but nothing past the first bend."

"And if I choose the wrong one, I'll be stuck . . ."

"Possibly."

"So how do you do it? How do you know what fork is the right one to choose?"

"The Lord knows, Mercy. The Lord knows the plans He has for you, plans for good and not evil. But He won't tell them to your head, you have to learn to listen to His voice in your heart."

"How do I do that?"

"You already are. You've heard His voice, the way you rush into danger with a heart of compassion; that's His voice compelling you. It's when you obey, simply because your heart tells you it's what the Lord would want you to do, whether your mind agrees or not. Just continue to be faithful and obey, and He will guide your way."

"It sounds easy, but my anxiety over the matters of my future tell me it'd be simpler not to make any decisions and just live with you and Mama forever."

"Ha," Henry chuffed, slapping his knee. "As much as I'd love to keep you, you've got too big a destiny, Mercy. Do you remember what David told Goliath before he smote him with the stone? He said, I've killed a lion and a bear, and you will be no different. Mercy, with all the Lord has brought you through . . . I'd be in error not to let you go on to what's next with my full blessing. Sure, what you cannot see may, at the moment, seem daunting and scary, but so have many of the things you've already passed through. I'm excited to see where you will go and the difference you will make."

"So, you don't want me anymore?"

Henry chuffed, nudging her. "You know that's not true."

"I know," Mercy grinned.

"All that being said, I don't think we need to rush your departure," he said, putting an arm around her. "When the time comes . . . you'll be ready for it."

Mercy sat beside him until her eyes closed and her world faded to the sounds of the crackling fire. Her heart already had a home, and she was content, mostly. Still, she couldn't help but dream about what kind of life the Lord was preparing her to live. Henry was right, she was beginning to lose count of the lions and bears she'd endured, but she hoped what waited for her beyond the war was not a giant, but peace.

She was awakened for a moment as his strong arms lifted her gently from the stump, before returning to her dreams in the safety of his presence. If there were ever to be a man to capture her heart, his competition would not be amongst the other young men, but with this man. And right now, the competition wasn't even close.

Chapter 6

I'm telling you, Mr. Musgrave, it's better to get them up and moving about once they're able," Mercy argued.

"And the books say bedrest, lass."

"The books were written years ago, sir. Captain Davis's notes show a quicker recovery time for those who got up and moving periodically over those kept to their cots."

The early July sun already had the room feeling thick and muggy, only adding to the heat of the conflict. Mercy could feel sweat rolling down her neck.

"You've read the captain's notes?"

"Every one of them," Mercy said.

"Odd," Musgrave replied, scratching his beard. "You're a woman . . . and a young one at that."

"The captain and I were . . . close friends, and he wanted his knowledge to enhance my own."

"Hmmm," Musgrave mused. "I pray that you remember your place as well as you do his anecdotes."

"My place is to stand between these boys and the grave," Mercy said. "And I'll fight that battle the way Captain Davis taught me, with all that I am."

"You're a stubborn thing, aren't you? So be it, Miss Young. Get them up and moving, but should their condition digress, it'll be you who will have to make an answer."

"Thank you, sir." Mercy curtsied.

"Goodness, Mercy," Adelaide whispered as they returned to their patients. "I swear you'd take on a bear if you thought you were right."

"I only fight the battles I believe are necessary, but once I've crossed that line, I have no intention of surrendering."

A commotion of cheers outside disrupted their conversation and drew them to the door.

"What is it?" Adelaide asked.

"Heaven knows," Mr. Musgrave said. "Maybe the lobsterbacks gave up."

"Do you think it's possible?" Mercy gasped.

"What's the news?" Mr. Musgrave called out to a passing sergeant.

"The king of Spain, Charles the Third, has declared war on the British!" the sergeant replied.

"The redcoats' troubles are multiplying—both here and at home," Musgrave said. "They're about to find themselves backed into a corner."

While the news was good indeed, Mercy felt a measure of sorrowful pity as well. She wanted the British to leave America, but she didn't wish them to be annihilated. Britain was where her ancestors had come from, the reason she'd been born here, and she probably had many not-so-distant relations fighting for the other side. They were all kin, like Cain and Able, too proud to let one another live in peace.

"Well, come along then," Musgrave said. "The war isn't over yet.

How right Flint had been. Over the following two weeks, the British landed troops on the shores of Connecticut, taking Black Rock Fort on July 5th. Next, they attacked Fairfield on the 7th, burning fifty-four barns, forty-seven storehouses, eighty-three homes, two churches, and the jail and courthouse. This devastation was followed by an attack on Norwalk on the 11th, where General Tryon's soldiers burned eighty-seven barns, seventeen shops, and four mills.

Total damage done by the British was estimated at twenty-six thousand British pounds, and sparked outrage amongst local Patriots and Tories alike. Spies divulged that General Clinton hoped these malicious attacks would draw General Washington out of his fortified high ground and into a battle more favorable for the redcoats. Pressure on Washington rose as calls for retaliation and results mounted.

"We're going to be gone for a few days," Henry said. "We'll be under the command of General Wayne. You remember—the general from the Paoli Massacre?"

Mercy nodded as she swallowed a bite of fish they'd caught earlier.

"We were selected because of our marksmanship," Ben added. "We're marching out with the best in the army, a special new unit. We'll show the Brits they're not the only ones who know how to raid."

But his remark did little to dissuade the worried look in Adelaide's eyes.

"Where are you going?" Mercy asked.

"We can't tell you that," Henry said. "Orders."

"When are you marching?" she tried.

"We can't tell you that either." Henry frowned. "But Benjamin is right, we're marching out with the best and the redcoats don't know we're coming; we'll be alright."

Mercy nodded—for *his* sake.

Just then, a drummer's cadence rolled through the camp. Henry and Benjamin stood, setting down their plates.

"I guess that's the call," Henry said.

Mercy and Adelaide stood.

Henry reached out, pulling her into an embrace. "We'll be back in a few days, you'll see. We always come back, Mercy."

Mercy nodded; she knew her voice would crack if she dared speak.

For Adelaide it was too late. Ben did his best to console her, but at last it was Mrs. Bell who had to wrap her up so they could leave. Mercy watched until their forms faded out of the firelight, and they were gone. Sitting back on her stump, she noticed tears glistening on Mable's cheeks. She knew the pain of watching her papa march off to battle, never to return.

"There, there, girl," Mrs. Bell cooed. "All these tears aren't going to fetch him back now. We'd best set our mind to our prayers; they're in the Lord's hands now."

But this notion only broke Adelaide's heart all the more.

History would never record the suffering of this kind. The invisible wounds born by wives and children, parents, lovers, and friends. The agony of waiting in the lonely terror of the unknown with only one's awful thoughts as comfort, and a poor comfort they were.

Theo leapt from Mercy's shoulder, gliding to sit beside Adelaide, staring up at her with his big yellow eyes. Amongst her hitching breaths, Mercy watched a smile appear. Even Mrs. Bell had to smile at his obvious concern.

"I'll be alright," Adelaide said, looking down on him while she wiped her tears with the back of her hand. "He wouldn't want me to stay this way."

The following day, Mercy and Adelaide took the Bells and Abe on an adventure in the woods. They followed the stream for a while, stopping here and there to splash in the water or look for crayfish. Abe, too grown up in his own mind for such foolishness, looked on with apparent indifference, scanning the woods from time to time with his musket.

They'd wandered a ways from camp when they emerged from the trees at the edge of a clearing. Abe held up his hand to halt the band. Slipping his musket from his shoulder, he began to raise it.

"What is it?" Mercy asked.

"Shhh," Abe hissed. "Indians," he whispered, nodding towards the clearing.

Mercy's eyes drifted past him to a long hut of some kind covered in bark. Beside it a woman and two younger children looked at them wide eyed, only fifty paces away.

The woman motioned with her arm and her children moved to stand behind her. Then she held up her hand, either saying hello, or halt.

"It is alright," the woman said in good English. "We are Oneida. Friends."

Abe looked at Mercy, who reached up and pushed Abe's barrel away.

The woman smiled and motioned for them to come.

Uneasily, Mercy led the band into the clearing.

"Welcome," the woman said. "Where have you come from?"

"The camp, up on the ridge." Mercy motioned behind them.

The woman smiled kindly, nodding. "My husband is a scout."

The woman wore a cotton dress covered in small flowers with some sort of leggings under it. She had beautiful long black hair, and a necklace which appeared to be made of shells or something of the like. Her children, their copper skin hardly covered on account of the warm weather, peered around her wide eyed. Her manner was so kind that Mercy felt uncannily at ease.

"Would you like to eat with us?" she asked.

"I don't—" Abe began.

"We'd love to," Mercy said.

The woman smiled wide, motioning them to come closer. "I am called Talise. It means beautiful waters."

"It suits you," Mercy said. "I'm Mercy, I think it just means Mercy, and this is Adelaide, Mable, Nathaniel, and Abe."

"Would you like some help preparing the food?" Adelaide asked.

Mercy heard Abe grumble, but he slung his musket all the same.

As Mercy's eyes adjusted to the shadowed interior of the long house, she was surprised by how tidy it was. Animal pelts carpeted the floor except for an area near the middle where a fire ring filled with glowing coals sent wisps of smoke up and out of a hole in the ceiling. Over the fire hung a pot, much like the one they used in the camp, and inside a stew bubbled lazily.

"May I ask how you learned to speak English so well?" Mercy asked.

Talise smiled. "Many of the Oneida speak English and French because of the missionaries, but I learned it from my father, he was an English trapper. He was killed in the last war with the French, my mother will be along after a while, she is out in the forest foraging. May I ask you why you have an owl on your shoulder?"

"I rescued him," Mercy said. "He could leave but he just doesn't."

"She spoils him," Adelaide interjected.

"My people have a great respect for the owl," she said. "Many fear it as an omen of death."

"Would you like me to leave him outside?" Mercy asked. "Honestly, most times I forget he's even there."

Talise studied him for a moment. "He doesn't seem to bear any ill will," she said, cocking her head sideways to mimic him. "He's just—misunderstood—like we all are."

Mercy watched Talise cut up a root of some kind and add it to the stew.

"Your fathers are in the camp?" Talise asked, selecting a few green onions.

"Our fathers are dead," Adelaide said softly.

Talise stopped chopping. "So many fathers," she sighed.

"I guess that's something we all have in common . . ." Mercy said.

"But not *all* we have in common." Talise smiled, looking out the door where the Bells and her children chased one another, kicking a ball made of animal hides.

Mercy had a million questions she wanted to ask about the way they lived, what it was like to be an Indian woman, and of course, trapping.

"It's ready," Talise said finally.

Mercy held the bowls while Talise filled them, and Adelaide fetched the kids. Instead of sitting at a table, everyone sat on the furs on the floor. Abe offered to say grace, and Talise obliged, motioning for her children to bow their heads. She wondered if it was out of sincerity, or perhaps they were just accommodating them. Like white folks, many of the natives had their own religions, though she'd heard that many had accepted the Lord.

"This is really good stew," Nathaniel said, after taking his first bite.

"Mmmm," Mercy agreed. "What is it?"

"Bever, wild onions, wild rice, and a few other things." Talise smiled.

"That's a far cry better than what we get in the camp," Abe admitted.

"My mother taught me the recipe."

"I'd love to learn it myself," Adelaide said.

"I can teach you," Talise offered. "Everything is provided by the forest."

"I love trapping," Mercy confessed between bites. "Though I've never caught a bever."

"It isn't difficult," Talise said. "But I'm surprised your mother permits you to trap."

"My mama is dead too," Mercy said. "But we've been adopted, and times being what they are, our new mama sees the blessings of it."

She caught Talise's youngest staring at Theo, scarcely able to eat.

"Would you like to feed him?" Mercy asked, looking to the boy's mother to see if it was okay.

The boy shook his head, no.

"He knows the legends," Talise said.

"I understand," Mercy said. "This owl is special; he's actually saved my life."

"And my brother's," Adelaide added.

"How did it manage that?" Talise asked.

"The legends," Mercy smiled. "My adoptive papa told me the only thing as powerful as the truth is what people believe is the truth. Theo doesn't have any special powers, good or bad, but people's belief that he does gives him a power he couldn't possibly have on his own. Like the king. He's just a man, no better or worse than any other, but people's belief that he has power enables him to possess it."

"Sounds like a wise man, your papa."

"He is," Mercy agreed.

"Is it true that native girls hunt and fish, sometimes with babies on their backs?" Mable asked.

"Yes." Talise smiled. "Most of the time our men do the hunting, but it isn't uncommon for wives to work alongside their husbands trapping, fishing, and foraging. We use a board like this, to carry our babies on our backs while we work."

"It's beautiful," Mercy said.

"Your life seems so much more adventurous than what we have to look forward to," Mable mumbled.

"It's a hard and harsh life sometimes," Talise said. "Every way of life has its blessings and its curses. The only bad life is one we are ungrateful for."

"Yes, ma'am," Mable replied.

"Appreciate the meal, ma'am," Abe said. "But I think it's time we were heading back."

"Perhaps you could come to the camp and eat with us sometime," Mercy offered. "Our cooking's not quite as good as yours, but it's alright."

"Perhaps," Talise said, standing and taking their bowls. "It was nice to meet you all."

"It was a blessing to meet you," Mercy said.

"That was the best stew I ever had," Nathaniel said, handing her his bowl.

"Go in peace," Talise said as they started back to camp. "You are always welcome here."

Mercy thought to herself as they followed the stream back towards camp. Talise wasn't a savage at all, just different, and Mercy hoped she'd have the opportunity to visit again.

"Wait until Mama finds out we ate with an Indian," Nathaniel said.

Chapter 7

It was July 20th before Mercy heard the shouts of jubilation from outside the medical cabin at the camp in Middlebrook, New Jersey. Immediately, the two nurses looked at Flint with pleading eyes.

"Oh alright, off with you," he said, waving towards the door.

The two girls flung their aprons onto their hooks and dashed out the door.

"This part always has my stomach in knots," Adelaide said. "I feel sick."

Finding their way to the road, Mercy gasped as she caught sight of the endless rows of redcoats marching towards them under guard.

"There must be hundreds of them!" Adelaide exclaimed.

"Here," Mercy said, guiding Adelaide over to an empty flatbed.

Climbing aboard, she held out her hand and helped her friend up. Together, they scanned the faces of the Continentals marching on either flank of the prisoner column.

"Where are they going to keep such a number?" Mercy asked.

The column moved up the road lead by General Wayne and his staff on horseback. The whole camp turned out to celebrate the victory with cheering and waving of banners. It was a breathtaking display, a victory the likes the Americans had not experienced in over a year.

"At this rate, it'll take all day to find them," Adelaide groaned. "If they're here to be found."

"They're here, stop fretting. There's hardly a bandaged man amongst them. They must have taken the redcoats by surprise."

As the column passed in front of them, Mercy felt a sense of awe watching the victorious general ride proudly on his steed. A general whose own men had been surprised by the vile General Grey and burned in their beds, but General Wayne had seen fit not to retaliate in kind. His prisoners looked none the worse for wear.

She was proud of him. He'd proven himself to be the better man and his country the more honorable. He made her feel proud to be an American.

The column was nearly at its end, and Mercy's own anxiety was beginning to rise when one of the Continentals held up their hand as they marched, waving excitedly. Her heart leapt, and a wave of relief sent her emotions crashing down on her.

"It's Ben!" she choked.

Adelaide turned to look where Mercy was pointing and threw herself out of the wagon, clawing her way towards him.

Mercy watched through blurry eyes as Ben handed his rifle to Henry and met her, lifting her off the ground in a tight embrace. Mercy climbed from the wagon and waited as the column snaked past until Henry reached her. Leaning the rifles against the flatbed, he swallowed her in his arms.

"I knew you'd come back," Mercy sobbed.

He kissed the top of her head, holding her as she let go of the terrible weight she'd carried while they were away.

"I know you did," Henry whispered.

That evening as they sat around the fire, Henry and Benjamin regaled the Bells and Youngs with tales of the battle.

"It was a dark march," Benjamin started. "We had to put bits of paper in our caps or we'd've lost the man marching in front of us. My stomach was in knots the whole way, and my heart drummed at an alarming rate."

"We arrived below the fort at Stony Point at nearly midnight," Henry said. "General Wayne had sent Major Murfree on a diversionary assault on the British center, and Colonel Butler to attack the north flank. The moon was covered by thick clouds, but we could hear the waves lapping on the beach before us."

"There were so few of us to take a fort so well defended, but General Wayne assured us we were up to the task, that freedom demanded such noble feats as these," Ben added while Henry paused to light his pipe.

"By midnight, Major Murfree had been discovered and the battle was on. We could hear them shooting heavy and continuous as we set off into the waters with General Wayne, aiming to flank the fort from the south. The water was cool, and soaked us beyond the knee, but the general pressed on."

"The general sent men on ahead," Ben said, "only a few, with axes and picks to cut holes for us though the walls of wood. Forlorn hope, we called them. Once they were discovered, the British cannons were turned on us, but the approach was so steep, and our assent so swift, they were unable to have any affect.

"My whole body trembled as the cannonballs hummed overhead, sending up sprays of water as they hit the channel. I had to will my legs forward, for fear had frozen them in place."

"Then," Henry cut in, "at the lead, I saw General Wayne take a ricocheted musket ball to the head and go down, but there was no time to stop, we were in the thick of it. Colonel Febiger took command without hesitation, leading us through the stockades and into the fort as Colonel Butler's troops breached the north side."

"As we reached the top, our men cried out, 'The fort is ours! The fort is ours!'" Ben cheered, squeezing Adelaide's hand enthusiastically. "I've never felt anything like it! Relief and excitement, joy and sorrow, exhausted and yet wide awake. We'd succeeded."

"Murfree's men paid the highest price," Henry said. "We couldn't have done it without them. We lost fifteen, with more than eighty wounded. In the morning, General Washington rode out to meet us and look over the battlefield. He congratulated us for our heroic efforts and ordered us to plunder the fort."

"Why?" Abe asked. "Why not just keep it?"

"Our aim was never to keep it, but to strategically retaliate for the ruthless destruction of American properties in Connecticut. By taking the fort, we captured nearly five hundred and fifty redcoats, muskets, powder, food stores, medical supplies, and fifteen cannons that will be invaluable in battles to come. This defeat greatly added to the cost of the war, pushing the king ever closer to the point of retiring from this land."

"General Wayne must be counting his blessings," Mrs. Bell remarked. "To take a musket ball to the head and still be able to ride home in victory is nothing short of the Lord's mercies."

"Aye," Henry said. "He's a humble man, and humbler still after such a miraculous escape from death."

"Will you be staying in camp for a while?" Adelaide asked hopefully.

Ben looked over at Henry.

"It's difficult to say," Henry sighed. "We are often at the whim of the redcoats since our strategy here is a defensive one. While the British maintain the upper hand in the South, we must be cautious not to lose our advantage in the North or the war will be lost. Benjamin and I are deployed to keep the redcoats from gaining that advantage."

Adelaide nodded, though her downcast eyes could not hide her disappointment.

"We'll be given leave for a few days," Ben said. "We'll spend it together."

"Accompanied," Mrs. Bell interjected.

"Yes, ma'am," Benjamin said. "We'll be accompanied."

"I don't need my daughter becoming the root of some hideous camp scandal."

"No, ma'am," Ben replied. "I live to uphold her honor and good character."

"Live to honor the Lord, young Benjamin. A man that honors the Lord need never worry about anything else."

"Yes, ma'am."

Though she felt bad for him, Mercy was glad to have someone else around to garner some of Mrs. Bell's constant corrections.

Through the sounds of merriment echoing around the camp came the thudding sounds of approaching horse hooves. Everyone looked up as the muzzle of a horse appeared in the firelight.

"I'm here to fetch a nurse," the young rider said. "Doc Musgrave needs some assistance with some of General Wayne's men."

"Tell him I'll be right there," Mercy said.

"I'll escort you," Jonathan offered.

"I—" Mercy sighed. "Thank you, I'll be ready in a minute."

Walking to the wash basin, she splashed water on her face and washed her hands before drying them off. She'd made the trek to the hospital cabin plenty of times on her own, but . . . she'd promised.

"Ready," Mercy said.

As they walked, Mercy appreciated the darkness hiding any awkward nonverbal communication between them. She knew he was trying hard, and that this was part of the process of growing up. Young men would feel compelled to try and win her heart despite her discouragement, and she would feel compelled to endure it until they gave up.

"It's good to have your brother and father back," he said.

"It is," Mercy agreed.

"Sounds like they're heroes."

"Yes, it's good to have another victory."

"Looks like it runs in the family—capturing British, that is."

At first, she didn't know what he was talking about, but then it dawned on her, he was talking about the foraging party bathing in the river that she, Abe, and David had foolishly captured.

"Heh, yeah . . ." Mercy replied, a little embarrassed.

"It's hard being a line soldier sometimes," he said. "We don't get special orders or assignments. We're always standing in the middle. Just a mess of warm bodies until we're not. No one will ever call me, or my pa, a hero . . . When this is all over, no one will ever even know we were here."

Mercy could hear the heaviness in his voice. He wasn't wrong, she rarely thought about his part in the war, though his fellow soldiers and even his pa paid the same awful price. Their units were never publicly praised, or awarded a citation, they just . . . were. But without them the war would be lost, without them the special units couldn't do what they did. They were necessary, vital, and she felt ashamed that she hadn't even given it a thought before now.

"I'll remember you," Mercy said. "And I, for one, am eternally grateful you are here."

They arrived at the cabin and Jonathan gave her a gentle bow.

"Thank you for the escort," Mercy said, returning his bow with a curtsy.

He turned and set off again, back into the night.

She had little time to ponder their conversation as she entered the cabin. The room was filled with wounded soldiers on cots. Some had simple flesh wounds that only required a bit of cleaning and a bandage, while others drew raspy breaths as they fought for life at death's door.

Across the room she saw Flint hovering over a howling patient, attempting to extract a musket ball from his calf. Rushing to collect her apron, she threw it on, navigating her way through the maze of patients.

"Ahh, there you are," Flint said. "My stub is numb from all this standing, and my hands are shaky with fatigue."

"Take a rest," Mercy said, reaching for the forceps.

Musgrave relinquished them and hobbled over to his desk to massage his nub.

"I'm sorry about the pain," Mercy said. "Has he given you any ale?"

The man nodded.

"Alright. I have steady hands, sir. I'll get it on the first try. Bite down on that roll for me and keep your hands under your backside. I'll be through in a minute."

Centering her tool over the oozing hole, she inserted them until they reached the ball.

"Almost there," Mercy said. Widening the forceps in the tight channel, she carefully guided them around the ball and bit down. "Okay, I've got it. It's important you don't reach for me; we don't want to have to do this again."

As gently as possible, she lifted the ball from the hole and dropped it on a tray. The soldier gasped in relief.

"You were right brave, sir. I'm going to poor a little ale on your wound, it's gonna burn something fierce, but it'll clean it."

The man tensed as she bathed the hole in alcohol. Satisfied, she washed the area with a rag, dried it as best she could, and put a fresh bandage on it.

"Finished," she smiled. "It'll be sore for a good long while, but you'll be alright. Thank you for your part in the battle, you brought my papa and brother home safe."

"I'm afraid they like you a good bit more than they like me," Musgrave grumbled from his desk.

"Perhaps you should try putting on a dress," Mercy jested.

"HA! Haha," Musgrave laughed. "That would certainly distract them from the pain!"

A few cots over, Mercy noticed an Indian man with a lower abdomen wound that had yet to be seen. The man's skin was pale compared to what it ought to be. Standing from her patient, she made her way over to him and began assessing his injury.

"Not that one," Musgrave said. "See to our others first."

"Why is this man here?" Mercy asked.

"He's one of our scouts," Flint answered. "But we take care of our soldiers first."

Mercy's blood ran cold. Looking the man in the eyes, she asked, "Do you have a wife named Talise?"

The man's eyes widened, and he nodded.

Chapter 8

Tearing open the man's shirt, Mercy went to work, rolling him on his side to check for an exit wound.

"Miss Young, step away from that man at once! That's an order!" Flint growled.

Mercy breathed a sigh of relief, there was an exit. The wound oozed dark blood, but the smell wasn't off. She dipped a rag in her water bowl and began cleaning the area.

"Miss Young!" Flint barked, standing from his desk.

Mercy's teeth went on edge. Inhaling deeply through her nose, she stood from her patient and faced Flint at his desk. "I am NOT a soldier, Mr. Musgrave, I'm a human being, and you ought to be asking yourself when you stopped being one long before you start hollering at me," she said coldly. "I am going to treat this man right now! Or, so help me, I will never treat another!" she said, glancing around the room.

Flint's jaw clenched and his nostrils flared. "So be it, Miss Young, but if we lose one of these boys because of your negligence, it'll be on your head."

Mercy returned to her patient still seething and continued to clean the wound. "Would you like some ale for the pain?" she asked.

The man nodded and she handed him the flask.

"The ball passed through, it may have clipped your liver, but I think you have a fair chance if we get you cleaned up and bandaged properly. Sorry for the lack of respect, men have been finding reasons to look down on one another since Cain and Able. I've met your wife, she's beautiful and kind. She fed us the best stew I ever tasted; it had beaver in it. I'll be sure to send someone to let her know you're here and to make sure she has no trouble coming to you."

"Thank you," he winced, handing her back the flask.

Mercy took it and poured some on the wound. "I'm going to need you to sit up if you're able," she said, holding out her hand.

The man took it and with a little pull, got himself upright. Pulling off the man's shirt, she set it aside and poured more ale on the hole in his back. Fetching a roll of bandages, she wrapped him several times and tied it off.

Gently laying him back on the cot, she said, "Rest, if you're able. It takes a while to heal a wound of that kind."

He nodded, closing his eyes.

Mercy could feel Musgrave glaring as she cleaned up her rags.

"Were you this stubborn with the captain?" he asked.

"Worse," Mercy answered shortly, preparing for the next patient.

"He failed to mention *that* in his notes," Musgrave remarked gruffly.

Collecting her medical supplies, she moved on to the next wounded soldier.

The following morning, Mercy explained the situation with Talise's husband at breakfast. Though still on the fence about the natives, Mrs. Bell could appreciate a woman's need to know the welfare of her husband. Seeing the woman had treated her children with kindness, Mrs. Bell agreed that someone ought to return to the longhouse and inform her of the situation.

"Flint . . ." Mercy looked over at Mrs. Bell. "I mean, Mr. Musgrave won't allow me the time to deliver the news myself," Mercy said regrettably. "We've too many patients."

"I'll deliver the news for you," Jonathan volunteered. "Though I don't know the way."

"I know the way," Abe sighed. "But we have to be quick about it, I have horses to tend to."

"Thank you," Mercy said. "They're good people, and we ought to show them the same love and respect we'd show any of God's precious ones."

"May I go too?" Nathaniel asked. "I want to play with Kaniehtiio (Gun yeh dee yo) and Okwaho (Og-wah-ho) again!"

"Lord, would you have all my good work undone?" Mrs. Bell prayed, looking to the heavens.

"I think you should stay here this time," Jonathan said. "Abe is in a hurry, and we don't know how they will take the news."

When they'd finished breakfast, Abe and Jonathan collected their muskets and started for the woods while Mercy, Adelaide, and Mable cleaned up.

"I'm afraid Flint is going to be most disagreeable today on account of me," Mercy said as they scrubbed the dishes.

"It's fortunate we have so many patients to attend to," Adelaide said. "We'll be kept so busy, perhaps he'll forget the matter entirely."

"I hope so," Mercy yawned. "Because he hadn't by the time I departed last night."

"Do you really believe they're the same as us?" Mable asked. "I mean, they look and act so different, and I've overhead dozens of terrifying stories about them."

"I imagine they've heard many terrifying stories about us too. But you wouldn't want them to judge you based on the sins of other settlers and soldiers, and if the shoe was on the other foot, would you want to be judged on the color of your skin alone?" Mercy asked. "Or would you want to be judged for who *you* are apart from the sins of others of your same color?"

Mable thought for a moment. "I guess I'd want to be judged for who *I* am."

"As we all will be," Mrs. Bell said from behind them, causing Mercy to jump. "Regardless of the color of our skin."

"Then we ought to look at others the same way," Adelaide said.

Mrs. Bell nodded reluctantly, before turning and walking away.

"I didn't expect that," Mercy whispered.

"She's different now that Papa's gone," Adelaide said, watching her mother go. "She still acts stubborn, but her heart is raw and tender. This war has humbled all of us . . ."

Mercy and Adelaide worked diligently serving their patients, and to Mercy's surprise, Musgrave didn't say a word when she got to Talise's husband. He appeared to be asleep, but she noticed his color was still off. She felt his forehead with the back of her hand. It was warm.

Dipping a rag in cool water, she rung it out and placed it on his head. He stirred a little but didn't open his eyes.

"I told you it was a waste of time," Musgrave said in his gravelly voice.

"It's only a small fever," Mercy said, not turning.

"The wound's turning septic," Musgrave said. "I checked it this morning."

Mercy closed her eyes in a pleading prayer as she lifted his bandages. She saw the skin around the wound had a pinkish hue, and when she felt the area, it was uncharacteristically warm. She got down and smelled the wound. It smelled of dried blood but there was no foul odor yet.

"Wounds get warm when they're healing," Mercy replied. "And fever is common for a few days."

Musgrave shook his head, returning to his notes.

But she was worried. Mercy could count on one hand the number of patients who'd survived such a wound.

After about an hour, there was a commotion outside the door.

"Ma'am, I am not permitted to allow you—"

"It's alright," came Jonathan's muted reply. "Her husband is in there."

In a moment the door swung open, and Talise stepped inside with Jonathan on her heels. Her eyes scanned the room frantically until she found him.

"Tier?!" she cried, rushing across the room to him.

"Oh perfect," Musgrave grumbled glaring at Mercy. "If the squaw is going to make a fuss, she needs to take it outside. These soldiers need rest!"

"She's fine," Jonathan replied. "She's only just found out."

Mercy watched her kneel beside him, feeling his face. His eyes opened, and he smiled as he placed his hand on her face and spoke something in Oneida.

"They're with my mother," Talise answered in English.

He nodded, still stroking her hair.

Talise lifted the bandages, checking his wounds, her eyes swelling with tears.

Placing the bandages back in place, she stood facing Mercy. "I need to take him back with me, he needs good medicine."

"Medicine?" Musgrave chuffed. "You mean witchcraft."

She ignored him.

Mercy looked back at Tier, his face ashy with the battle his body was in.

"It's fine with me," Musgrave said. "Take him and do what you like."

"I can't carry him," Talise said, her eyes pleading.

"Ben is on leave," Jonathan said. "We can get him there."

"He'd be glad to do it," Adelaide agreed.

"Thank you," Talise said, turning back to her husband.

In thirty minutes, Ben and Jonathan had Tier on a gurney and were headed out the door.

"Satisfied?" Musgrave asked. "Better he's buried with his own people than with ours."

Mercy stepped to reply, but Adelaide caught her arm. Swallowing the cross words dangling at the tip of her tongue, she turned to her patients. Adelaide was right, it was no use arguing with a person who wasn't open to persuasion. Tier was sure to receive better care at home where he was loved, than to suffer here under contempt.

There was truly a blindness present, even amongst those fighting for freedom, a blindness not of the eyes, but of the heart. Man judges by the outward appearance, while the Good Lord judges according to the heart. It saddened Mercy to see folks so willing to lay down their lives for a cause, and yet miss the heart of the cause in the process.

The war wouldn't solve everything. Hard hearts would always find reasons to look down on others, only the love of God could cure that. She prayed for Flint, that he'd put himself in Talise's shoes and find compassion. They were all just people. They dreamed the same, worked the same, loved the same, and hurt the same.

When the day finished, Mercy and Adelaide returned to the wagon to join the rest of their families. The day had been an emotional one, and Mercy was eager to hear how the trip with Tier had gone. When they arrived, they found Henry, Ben, Nathaniel, and Abe playing a game of whist while Mable helped Mrs. Bell prepare supper.

Henry rose from his stump and gave Mercy a hug. "Have a long day?" he asked.

"Yes, though tomorrow should be better. The more severely wounded are being sent to hospitals to recover, we'll only be left with those likely to return to service."

"I hear you've made friends with the Oneida," Henry said.

"With one," Mercy replied. "Her husband was a scout for the army, but he's been gravely wounded."

"He's the last man in their family," Ben said. "But Talise assured us she's strong enough to maintain their camp with her mother's help. Jonathan and I are of the mind to fetch her some game, seeing she's a friend of yours."

"She's a kind woman," Mercy said. "Her husband would probably fare better if she were able to stay by his side, though with a wound like that, his odds aren't good."

"You did the best you could, Mercy," Adelaide said. "He'd have no odds if you hadn't been there."

"Well, we should all pray for him then," Henry said. "God shows no partiality."

"Amen," Mrs. Bell agreed.

Chapter 9

July 25, 1779

   Captain Tobias Davis,

   My dear friend, your last letter arrived as a godsent ray of sunshine on a particularly bitter day. Your kind words of affection and hope were like a balm to my soul which longs to be anywhere but here. We are all alive and well, and as you said, that is cause enough for rejoicing. Sometimes in the midst of trials I forget to acknowledge my blessings, and I count your friendship amongst the chiefest of those.

   Tier, the brave Oneida warrior whose scouting guidance aided us in victory at Saratoga and Stony Point, through bitter struggle with infection, has passed. Why his loss has burdened me so utterly deeply I cannot explain. Perhaps it is because even though he was misunderstood, and even mistreated, by folks like us, he still chose to see the virtue of our cause and fight selflessly alongside us all the same.

Talise, his wife, of whom I wrote to you, has borne the loss with tremendous courage, though I know the pain she will ever carry in her heart. She is resolved to care for her family, though wars have taken every man amongst them. I grieve for her young children who will have to walk this difficult world without a father and pray to God that a man as noble as Henry would come and fill that place. I did all I could, I know that in my heart, but my soul still finds itself bitterly disappointed in my feeble efforts.

Our work is so desperate at times, I find myself emptied of hope, but then, by God's grace, a fever breaks, a wound heals, and a soldier rises from his bed. And I'm reminded, for that man, for that family, I have been blessed to make a difference. I pray that you and the Lord will forgive me for my weaknesses and lack of faith; I ever strive to be better.

A terrible battle occurred northwest of our camp here at Middlebrook on the 22nd. A militia of Iroquois and Tories set about raiding Patriot settlements in hopes of further aggravating our command. The local militia was called to provide relief but were ambushed on the road. No quarter was given, and forty-six men perished. General Clinton is truly a merciless man, and his brutal tactics to draw out General Washington at the cost of civilians will tarnish his reputation forever. We will not forget.

In spite of the redcoats' best efforts, our cause remains surer than ever, and the boys are itching to match the redcoats on the field when it seems wisest to do so. The men train with conviction, and each day our position becomes more secure. Henry says General Clinton's desperate actions only prove the redcoats know their time here is short. All we need to do is hold the line.

Rumors have been circulating around camp that an American navy expedition set sail from Boston yesterday to reclaim the coast of Maine. I've heard it is over one thousand soldiers and forty-four ships; it appears we've grown tired of waiting on French promises. If our navy can secure victory in Maine, then perhaps we can take control of the sea and cut off British resupply. The end of the war may yet be in sight.

I pray every day that the Good Lord would surprise us all and bring this war to a close. I look forward with anxious anticipation for your return to the North so we can resume our friendship face to face once more. I will forever be grateful for that long night on Dorchester Heights.

Affectionately,

Mercy Young

"What on earth, Theo!" Mercy exclaimed as she climbed out of the wagon.

There on the buckboard, sitting proud as could be, was her owl, clutching a British officer's wig in his talons.

Mrs. Bell let out a snort. "Do you think he snatched it while it was on or off the officer's head?"

"On, I hope," Mercy laughed, trading him a bit of dried fish for the wig.

"Could you imagine that surprise?" Mrs. Bell said. "And how will he explain when he shows up to muster and it's missing?"

"I wish I could've seen it," Adelaide said. "I hope it was General Clinton's."

"Hear, hear," Mrs. Bell said.

"What do I do with it?" Mercy asked.

"Hang it from the wagon like the heathen do their scalps," Mrs. Bell said, and then promptly clapped her hand over her mouth.

Adelaide burst out laughing. "Mama!" she exclaimed.

Mrs. Bell turned red as a turnip.

"And what has you ladies in an uproar?" Jonathan asked, coming from his unit's cabin for breakfast.

"Theo snatched himself a British officer's wig and Mama thinks we ought to hang it from the wagon like a scalp," Adelaide laughed again.

Jonathan eyed his mother in disbelief before bursting out laughing himself. "Oh, how this war has changed us all."

"It was a slip of the tongue," Mrs. Bell said curtly, in her defense. "This war has gone and made me a little salty is all, and I've got good reason."

"Hear, hear," Jonathan agreed. "Though I feel taking scalps may be taking it a little too far."

"It was a slip of the tongue," Mrs. Bell muttered again.

"Here," Mercy said, handing the wig to Jonathan. "Maybe one of your officers can use it."

"What have you ladies planned for the day?" Jonathan asked.

"After our rounds, Adelaide and I are taking your siblings to see Talise. Kaniehtiio and Okwaho could use the distraction, and I'm sure Talise, strong and stubborn as she is, could use the help," Mercy said.

"Would you mind if I tag along?" Jonathan asked. "I have no orders today."

"Sure," Adelaide said. "Many hands make light work."

As they wandered down the wooded path that followed the stream to the clearing which Talise called home, Mercy's heart was heavy. Tier had passed away only two days ago, leaving an impossible hole in the lives of his family. But when things got hard, Americans pulled together.

Abe and Jonathan had brought canes for fishing, and as they walked beside the cool crystal water of the stream, Mercy wished she had too. Theo also seemed a little disappointed and annoyed that his ride had not remembered to bring along the means to his

satisfaction, and Mercy had no doubt that once they arrived at the clearing, he'd abandon her in favor of his stomach.

The thudding of an axe reached them long before they stepped out into the clearing and saw Talise busy splitting wood near the longhouse while her children took turns trying to stack it. In a kinder world she'd have time to grieve, but that was not her world.

Looking up in alarm as she caught sight of them, her muscles relaxed as familiarity dawned and she set down her axe.

"I hope it's alright we stopped by," Mercy said as they walked up. "Nathaniel and Mable were itching to see your young ones again, and Adelaide and I thought maybe we could be of some help."

"You are always welcome," Talise said with a warm smile, wiping her forehead with the back of her hand.

"If it's alright, ma'am, Abe and I can finish this wood for you," Jonathan offered.

Talise sighed. "Only if you'll stay for dinner."

"Yes, ma'am," Jonathan nodded.

Talise dismissed her children to play with the Bells.

"How can we help?" Mercy asked.

"It's been days since I've been in the garden," she said. "The weeds grow fast this time of year."

"Lead the way," Mercy smiled.

Talise led them around the longhouse to an impressive garden and in minutes the ladies were surrounded by head high cornstalks ringed with pole beans. Mercy had to be careful where she stepped to avoid the squash vines that ran along the ground.

"We call them the three sisters," Talise said. "The corn provides a stalk for the beans to climb, and the squash covers the ground to shade the weeds."

"That's genius," Mercy said.

"It was handed down by my ancestors," Talise replied.

"If the army doesn't move, do you think I could trap with you this fall and winter?" Mercy asked. "You have much more knowledge than I have, and I'd like to learn to do it your way."

Talise thought for a moment. "Things *are* going to be more difficult now." She frowned. "Having help would be a blessing."

"You seem so young," Adelaide said. "I can't imagine the load you must carry."

"I'm twenty," Talise said, pulling up a weed. "Tier and I were married when I was fifteen."

"You've been taking care of a family since you were fifteen?" Mercy asked, wide eyed.

"Yes, it is our people's way. Young Oneida women are usually married by the time they are fifteen to eighteen. Our husbands are often a year or two older."

"I can't imagine," Mercy sighed. "I don't feel I'll ever be ready."

"I don't think anyone feels ready," Talise said. "But once that is where you are, you just do it, and it comes surprisingly natural."

"That's what my mama said too," Adelaide said.

"Do you enjoy being a mother?" Mercy asked.

"There's nothing like it," Talise said. "Without my children I feel I'd be lost without Tier, but they give me a reason to rise, to keep working, keep hoping, and make myself better. They are counting on me, and the love I feel for them . . . it's deep inside, like a hunger. I long for them and their future, that it would be bright, and I will work hard to make it so. And it is a lot of work," she laughed tiredly.

"They are full of energy and curiosity," Mercy agreed.

"How old are you?" Talise asked.

"I'm seventeen," Adelaide said. "And Mercy will be seventeen in October."

"Neither of you are married?"

"Hopefully soon," Adelaide smiled. "As soon as the war is over."

"Ahh, your man is a soldier," she smiled. "And you?" she asked Mercy.

"No . . . maybe someday. I know that's what everyone expects, I just . . . I just don't feel ready for it."

"The heart is a delicate thing, and yours, like so many others, has been wounded many times. It may be that it needs time to heal before it is ready to entrust itself to another once more. It is a painful thing to lose someone you love, but if to avoid pain we never love, we miss the meaning of being alive. Love is rich and powerful because of the risk and sacrifice, and a life of love is the most meaningful life, though it may also be the most painful."

"So, you would still have married Tier, even if you knew beforehand that he would die?" Mercy asked.

Talise nodded her head, thoughtfully. "Even though I only had him for a little while, our love made our life rich, and I would be the poorer if we hadn't. The pain I feel now is only proof of how well I was loved, and it too is part of the richness of life."

"But sometimes it hurts so much." Mercy swallowed hard.

"Yes," Talise said, wrapping her arms around her.

By the time they'd concluded their weeding, Abe and Jonathan had already finished splitting and stacking the firewood. Seeing that everyone was wet with sweat and plenty dirty, they headed to the stream to fish and splash the afternoon's labors away.

While the ladies sat dipping their feet into the water, Jonathan hooked into a good fish and handed his cane to Okwaho who'd been watching him with excited anticipation. The fish pulled hard for the deeper water of the channel, dragging Okwaho towards the edge. Taking a knee, Jonathan wrapped an arm around his waist to hold him as the battle continued.

Behind them, Kaniehtiio jumped up and down, leaning this way and that as her brother fought to hold on to the cane. Mercy smiled with delight at their excitement; fishing always made her feel the same way.

In a few moments Jonathan helped Okwaho lift a nice trout from the stream. Ruffling the boy's hair, he took the fish and slid it onto a long thin birch branch.

"That's a good one, boy," Jonathan said. "We'll rebait your hook and go after another."

Okwaho grinned as he struggled to lift the stick and show his mother his catch.

"Well done!" Talise cheered.

And in that moment, Mercy understood what Talise had meant. She wouldn't trade this moment for a pain-free life, she wouldn't trade it for anything.

Chapter 10

The war in the North had turned into a bit of a stalemate. While no word had arrived from Maine on the American navy's exploits, Washington's spies revealed that British General Clinton was struggling to get enough supplies and soldiers to make any headway beyond holding New York now that the French and Spanish had entered the war.

Washington waited patiently, not wanting to foolishly risk his army on an attack that may not be necessary nor guaranteed when time itself might win the war without further losses. The two armies glared at one another through spyglasses, willing the other to make a mistake.

While the main armies kept one another in check, things on the frontier were far less mundane. In late July a combined army of three hundred native Seneca warriors and one hundred British regulars laid siege to a fort in central Pennsylvania called Freeland Fort.

The one hundred and twenty-one settlers who'd taken refuge in the fort fought until they were out of ammunition and were forced to surrender. Twenty-one of them didn't survive. A relief party led by Captain Hawkins Boone on July 28th attempted to rescue the settlers but were overpowered by the larger attacking force and had to retreat after losing eighty-four of their own. It was the greatest American defeat suffered on the Pennsylvania frontier.

***

Mercy caught Henry grinning to himself at breakfast. For the past couple of days, he'd been acting awfully funny, and when she'd inquired as to why, he acted like she'd seen things. And there was more; every time horse harnesses jingled, or wagon wheels churned, he'd look about expectantly, only to return to his pipe looking somewhat disappointed.

The morning at the hospital had been slow, and as was often the case, Mercy had found herself talking to Theo as she stirred bandages in the cauldron. Henry's antics over the past few days had begun to rub off, and she found herself looking with anticipation at every wagon coming or going, though she didn't know what it was she was looking for.

She was in the process of hanging the rags when the sound of a wagon caught her attention. Although she was curious, she continued to hang bandages until the approach of trotting feet caused her to whip around in alarm. Young arms flung around her up as the boy's momentum nearly lifted her off her feet.

"Mercy!" David cried.

As her shock gave way, she wrapped him up in her arms.

"I've missed you so much!" he said, not letting go.

"I've missed you too!" Mercy said, kissing the top of his head. "Where did you come from?!"

"We've been in the wagon for DAYS!" he said. "Ben came and got us."

"So *that's* the secret mission he's been on," Mercy said.

"Mama wanted it to be a surprise!" David said.

"Well, I'm surprised. Where is Mama?"

She's in the wagon, Ben is going to park it next to the Bell's."

"David!" Adelaide cried, rushing over to him and wrapping him up as soon as he let go of Mercy.

"Did you know about this?" Mercy asked her friend.

Adelaide smiled sheepishly.

"We agreed, Adelaide. No secrets!" Mercy pouted.

"Mr. Henry asked me not to tell you," Adelaide pleaded, releasing David and taking her hands. "What choice did I have?"

"So, I was the only one kept in the dark?" Mercy asked.

"Only to make their arrival more special," Adelaide said. "It's impossible for Ben to keep secrets from me."

Mercy sighed. "Alright. Let's see if Flint will give us the afternoon off."

When Mercy arrived at the wagons after finishing with the bandages, Abigail was already sitting beside Henry gazing at him longingly as he cooed to Mary-Beth in his arms.

"Secret mission?" Mercy said, walking up.

Abigail jumped from her seat, swallowing Mercy in an embrace.

"Ahh yeah," Henry replied. "Of sorts."

"Let me look at you," Abigail said, letting her go. "My what a beautiful woman you're growing up to be. I think about you by the hour and pray over you nearly as often. It's been such a long time."

"It has, Mama," Mercy said, hugging her again. "How long will you be here?"

"Perhaps until the cold drives us out, or the redcoats surrender, bless God," Abigail said. "The war is at a standstill, and conditions here are not so poorly."

"Not at all," Mercy agreed.

"Would you like to hold her?" Abigail asked.

"Yes, please," Mercy replied.

"But . . ." Henry complained.

"You'll get another turn," Abigail chided.

Reluctantly Henry handed over the baby to Mercy.

"My, she's grown," Mercy said.

"She eats well," Abigail said. "And I do believe Mr. Hadley slips her sweets when I'm not looking."

Mercy felt warm all over as Mary-Beth wrapped her tiny fingers around Mercy's pinky. She was much pudgier than the last time Mercy had seen her, making her even softer and more adorable than before. Her curious eyes darted about taking in the scenery, and her tiny lips smacked playfully.

"I wish we could just get the war over with," Abigail sighed as she watched them. "I'm ready to be a family again."

"Aye," Henry agreed.

"Have you been on any adventures, Mercy?" David asked.

"A few," Mercy answered. "We met an Oneida woman and her two children, Okwaho and Kaniehtiio. They live just over the ridge and down the creek a bit."

"You're friends with an Indian?" he asked.

"Sure. She's kind, and her children are a lot of fun. You'd like them, Dave. Her husband was wounded and died a little while ago, it's just her and her mother now. She's going to let me trap with her this fall."

Abigail looked at Henry.

"I see no harm in it," Henry said. "They're good people. Got us out of that scrape up in Oriskany."

"You'd like her, Mama," Mercy said. "She's got a big wise heart just like you."

"Alright, you've had her long enough," Henry said, holding out his arms. "Give her back."

After a soft peck on the forehead, Mercy handed Mary-Beth back to him.

She wanted to cry—and to laugh—she wanted to run, and yet she felt exhausted. She hadn't been prepared for this, to be together again, everyone in one place, her family. It really had been so long.

Walking over to where Ben and Adelaide stood, held captive in each other's gaze, she punched him on the shoulder.

"Secret mission!" she fumed in feigned indignation. "I stayed up late every night praying for you!"

"Thank you," Ben winced, rubbing his shoulder.

"I can't trust either of you," Mercy huffed, eyeing them.

"To be fair, that's what Henry called it," Ben said.

Mercy chuffed. "I'll be having words with him later."

"It's good to have them back, isn't it?" Ben said. "You don't really understand how much you've missed them until they're here."

"Yeah . . ."

"Have you heard any word how we're fairing in Maine? It was a grand sight to see our navy sail out of the harbor in Boston," Abigail said.

"We've heard nothing," Henry replied.

"I hope we achieve a grand victory," Abigail added. "Show those Frenchmen what the American navy can do."

"I know what Captain Davis would say," Mercy frowned.

"He'd say those British buggers are better at sea and the odds are we'll be bested. Then he'd go poke a boil just so he can describe it's dreadful oozing in his journal," Abigail chuffed.

"Exactly," Mercy frowned.

"Have you heard from him?" Abigail asked.

"It's been a couple weeks since I've received any post," Mercy said. "And it's always so long in coming. But his last letter had him in generally good spirits, though he is lonely for us all. The war in the South goes much like it did here in the beginning, but with the passing of time, they are improving."

"And how is his replacement?" Abigail asked.

Mercy looked woefully at Adelaide.

"He's . . . learning," Adelaide said confidently.

"Aren't we all," Abigail said. "Well, he's blessed to have two girls as fine as you to aid him." Abigail sighed heavily, taking it all in.

Mercy knew the emotions she felt; after five grueling years of war, they were still together, safe and well, she didn't want anything more than that.

Mary-Beth began to fuss, forcing Henry to relinquish her to Abigail who disappeared into the wagon to feed her. Mercy watched the pride in Henry's eyes as he watched her go, it was a good kind of pride. He was proud of his resilient wife and their resilient family. And Mercy was too.

"Argh! Theo! That's mine!" David shouted.

Everyone turned to see David clambering up into the Bell's buckboard chasing Theo who appeared to have something furry held in his clutches.

"What's the matter, Dave?" Benjamin asked.

"It's a surprise!" David grunted as he lunged for Theo, just missing him.

"Whatever it is, you're going to have to trade him for it," Mercy said sympathetically.

"Here," Ben said, walking over and handing Abe a bit of fish from their supper.

"Daft bird hasn't changed one bit," David fumed, taking the fish.

"It isn't daft if it's working," Henry said, shaking his head in amusement.

David held up his hand and Theo took the fish, letting go of the object in his talons. Picking it up, David climbed out of the wagon and brought it over for everyone to see.

"It's a coonskin cap," David said proudly. "I caught him lurking in the storehouse behind the tavern and Mr. Hadley let me shoot him. Look, you can still see the hole right here," he said, poking his finger through the cap.

"That's a beautiful cap," Mercy said, petting it with her hand. "Looks warm too."

"It is," David said. "Although when it's windy I can feel it cause of the hole."

"I could sew it for you," Mercy offered.

"No . . . I like having the hole there," David smiled.

"Maybe tomorrow we could all go on an adventure once Adelaide and I are finished with our rounds," Mercy offered.

"I've got stalls to clean," Abe grumbled. "There's going to be an inspection."

"I can help," David offered.

For the first time all night, Abe smiled. "I sure would appreciate it."

"It must be hard work serving in the army," David said.

"I'm not in the army," Abe huffed.

"Sure, you are," Henry said. "And in a few months, you'll be old enough to ride as a dispatch rider like Ben did. Every job is important. If those horses aren't cared for, we don't have a cavalry, and without a cavalry, we'd have been flanked many a time by now. You've got to let yourself understand that this army is much more than the men pulling the triggers. It takes everyone."

"No one writes about stable boys," Abe said, tossing a stick into the fire.

Chapter 11

I'm so mad at him I can a hardly think straight!" Mercy blurted.

"Good heavens, Mercy. Captain Davis never even said a word," Abigail balked.

"But he would have, and you know it!" Mercy said, breaking a branch over her knee and tossing it into the fire.

Word had arrived in camp on the 20th of August that the American navy's Penobscot Expedition had utterly failed to achieve their objective in Maine. They suffered the loss of all of their ships and nearly five hundred soldiers as they fled overland to reach the safety of Boston.

"They couldn't even sink one ship?!" Mercy fumed. "Ugh, and Captain Davis would simply say our navy is but in its infancy, and theirs has been ruling the seas for decades. It is simply unrealistic to expect victory," she added in her best smug Captain Davis voice.

"And he'd be right, Mercy. I'm as disappointed as you are, but blaming the captain for our losses is like judging a man for sins he never committed," Abigail said, rocking Mary-Beth in her arms.

"Everything we're doing is in its infancy," Mercy groaned. "Our country is an infant!" she said, throwing up her hands.

"Yes, it is," Abigail agreed. "But we're learning from our losses as well. It's not us who's surrounded in New York, and if the redcoats thought they could whoop us, they'd be up here right now doing it."

Mercy broke another branch and tossed it into the fire.

"I think the captain is as disappointed as we are about these sorts of losses, but he's learned to temper his hope with the realities of what we've already faced."

"I was *going* to write him today . . ." Mercy mumbled.

"And why shouldn't you?"

"And what?! Confess he was right again without even being here to be right about it?!" Mercy chuffed.

"And confess that you miss him and think of him fondly," Abigail said.

"What?! Think of him fondly?" she scoffed.

"My girl. If you didn't think of him so fondly, he could never get you so flustered as you are . . ."

Mercy looked at her, trying to find the reason in her words.

"I was a young lady once too, remember. It is *because* you hold him in such high regard, his opinions, real or imagined, affect you so."

Mercy looked into the fire for a moment. "It's because I'm *fond* of being right, his opinions bother me so," Mercy replied with a half-smile.

"That poor man probably lives in trepidation of the day you ever are . . ." Abigail mused.

"It looks like we'll have to depend on the French, should they ever return, to beat the British at sea." Mercy frowned.

"Henry tells me to remember that while the French may not be present here, they are engaging the British elsewhere, and that in itself is helping our cause. British reinforcements and navy are being spread thin with all the conflicts here and in the West Indies. Were they not, surely we'd be having a rougher go of it."

"That's what makes losing even more humiliating . . ." Mercy groaned.

"It must be a most frightening thing to die at sea," Abigail reflected. "There wouldn't be much hope after a ship's gone under . . . no one can swim that long."

Mercy didn't like thinking about it. "Would it be alright if I took David to meet Talise and her children?" she asked.

"I don't see the harm in it," Abigail said. "But be back in time to help with supper."

"I will," Mercy said, leaning over to give Mary-Beth a kiss.

"It's nice to meet you, David," Talise said as Mercy introduced them outside the longhouse. "We were just about to go blackberry picking, would you like to join us?"

"Yes, ma'am," David replied, bowing slightly. "And it is nice to meet you as well."

"Where is Adelaide?" Talise asked.

"My brother is back so she's reluctant to part from him," Mercy replied.

"I understand." Talise nodded.

They gathered a few woven baskets and started for the woods with Okwaho and Kaniehtiio in tow. Finding a good patch, Mercy and Talise set down their baskets and together they began filling them with plump, juicy, delicious blackberries.

"Keep an eye out for bears," Talise said. "We're not the only ones who enjoy berries."

"Bears?!" David whimpered.

"Yes, bears," Talise said, a little surprised at his reaction.

"He was chased up a tree by a sow a couple of years ago . . . she nearly got him."

"You were chased by a bear?!" Okwaho asked.

"It happened during a game of hide and seek," Mercy said.

"I'd love to hear the story," Talise said, dropping a handful of berries into the basket.

"I don't know if I can," David said dramatically. "But if you insist."

Mercy looked up at Talise, rolling her eyes and shaking her head.

"Well, like Mercy said, we were playing hide and seek," David began. "Everyone else was hiding in all of the obvious places: bushes, behind trees, Abe even climbed up in one, but the leaves were already falling so that wasn't a good idea."

"So, where did you hide?!" Okwaho asked.

"Well, like Abigail always says, I'm a clever boy—"

"And modest too," Mercy butted in.

David shot her a glance. "I was the last to find my spot. I searched and searched until I found the perfect place where no one would find me. A tree had fallen over, roots and all, leaving a cave-like hole in the ground under the tangled mess of roots and branches. So, I tiptoed over to it, trying not to disturb the leaves so nobody would hear me, and I slipped inside."

"It does sound like a good spot," Talise agreed.

"It was," David said. "Until something started chuffing behind me in the darkness."

Okwaho gasped.

"Then it moved," David said dramatically, his eyes wide.

Okwaho gasped again.

"And it was big . . ." David said, clutching his own heart. "My heart started beating so hard and fast I thought it was gonna drum right out of my chest. I scrambled out of the hole and started running, then I heard the dry roots cracking as the beast emerged from its den."

"Were you scared?!" Okwaho asked, wide eyed.

"I was terrified like I've never been in my life!" David said. "And I've been in a scrape or two in my time."

Okwaho nodded, fixated on the storyteller.

"I looked over my shoulder and that big ol' bear was coming after me. I only had a moment to decide what I was going to do, and then I saw it, the perfect tree. It was fairly skinny, much too skinny for the bear to climb, but young and strong too. It had branches I could reach and pull myself up with quick."

Okwaho nodded his approval of David's choice.

"I darted for the tree as quick as my legs would carry me and began to climb, I'd only made it just out of reach when the bear hit the tree, nearly throwing me out of it."

The young boy gasped again.

"I wrapped my legs and arms around the trunk and cried for help. All the while that bear was clawing and thrashing my tree, I thought for sure she was going to rip it from the ground."

"That's when we heard him," Mercy said. "We'd already found everyone else by the time we heard his cries; we could tell he was in trouble. Abe was the first to find him, hanging on for dear life in that skinny little tree."

"Then what happened?" Okwaho asked.

"We sent everyone back with Adelaide to find help while Abe and I tried to figure out what to do. Before the game we'd been collecting chestnuts, and Abe got the idea of fetching them and throwing them at the bear to distract her."

"Your idea was to throw nuts at a bear?" Talise guffawed.

"Yeah . . . It does seem a little foolish now. But in the moment, with her cubs a few trees over wailing and her shaking that tree while David was wailing . . . we had to do something. I tried throwing a nut, but I'm no good at it, Abe on the other hand hit her on the first try. Then he hit her a second time, and that got her attention. She turned to face us."

"Oh goodness . . ." Talise said.

Mercy nodded. "Abe told me to hold out my dress and make myself look really big while we both yelled at the bear."

"You yelled at a bear?!" Okwaho gasped.

"Mmhmm," Mercy nodded. "And we must have looked and sounded something awful because that bear called her cubs down out of the tree and they dashed off into the woods like they'd seen a ghost," Mercy said.

"I've never been more relieved in my life," David said.

"That is some adventure," Talise said. "I don't think we need to worry about that happening here. As long as we keep talking and making noise, the bears ought to avoid us."

"Good," David said.

The berries were delicious, and Mercy couldn't help but pop a few into her mouth every now and again. She didn't much care for gardening, it felt like a chore, but foraging—now that was an adventure. There was always more to learn, and it felt like a treasure hunt that changed with the seasons. Food just waiting to be found, not sown or weeded—not by human effort anyway—but there it was, a buffet of good things to eat. Nuts and berries, plants and fungi, and even fish, fowl, and other meat.

There were so many ways to preserve food as well. Meats and cheeses could be smoked or kept in salt, some meat was cut into thin strips and dried over the fire, fish too were often dried or smoked. Roots could be hung in dark dry places; herbs too were hung and dried. Sometimes food was put in jars with a little salt which were then sealed with lard for weeks or months until the food was needed.

She'd already learned so much, and yet there was so much she had yet to learn. Each person she met was their own library of knowledge and experience, and if she was fortunate enough, they'd share it with her.

"You know," Talise said. "When my mother was a little girl, she had a scrape with a bear as well."

"Grandma?" Okwaho asked.

"Yes, she and my grandfather were checking the fish traps in the fall, not far from here. It was early in the morning, and they had many traps to check. They'd gone a good distance down the creek with good success, my grandfather's fish basket was beginning to fill up. He sent my grandmother a short way ahead to check another trap alone."

"How old was she?" Mercy asked.

"Oh, I think around eight or nine," Talise answered thoughtfully. "As she approached the trap, she heard thrashing and splashing in the water, and then she saw it, a gaunt old bear, wrestling with their trap. His face was scarred, his ear torn, and an eye clouded over where a rival's paw had put it out. She froze in her tracks as the old warrior caught sight of her and rose from the water on its hind legs."

"That must have been terrifying," David said.

"The two of them studied one another for several moments as water dripped from the bear's fur and jowls. My grandfather rounded the bend, and seeing them, raised his spear. But something washed over him, and as he studied the creature, he saw it was not intending harm but was simply starving and looking for an easy meal. Feeling a sense of compassion for the old warrior, he lowered his spear and walked carefully over to my mother. Setting down his basket, he took out a couple of the larger fish and threw them onto the shore near the bear."

"He didn't kill him?" David asked.

"There was no need," Talise said. "The bear wasn't going to harm them, and they'd have received little benefit from killing such an old bear."

"What happened next?" Mercy asked.

"The bear lowered itself on all fours and padded over to the fish. As it picked one up in its mouth, my mother saw that most of its teeth were missing. She learned a powerful lesson from her father that day. Just because one has the power to take a life doesn't mean one should. Her father respected the bear as one warrior does another, and perhaps in a way, he saw himself in the old bear, one day he too would be old and grey and need someone to help him gather food as well. None of us stay young forever."

"He sounds like a wonderful man," Mercy said. "Wiser than most."

"He was," Talise agreed. "I know this world would grieve his kind spirit. He thought nothing of empires or kingdoms, the notion that one man ought to rule another would be foreign to him as it ought to be to all of us. Each man ought to trouble himself with his own path and leave another's well enough alone. But," she sighed, "the world is changing . . ."

"What became of the bear?" David asked.

"I suppose it didn't survive the winter in its condition," Talise said. "But it died with my grandfather's respect."

David nodded.

Chapter 12

August 19, 1779

Captain Tobias Davis,

I wanted to begin this letter with an apology for my terse words in the last. It's not fair to lay the blame for our abysmal naval display at your feet, though I know you would have been right yet again. Henry says it's best to tell the truth rather than play shrewd games, and the truth is I miss you. I miss our talks and your understanding ear. I miss our banter in the field hospital that would lessen the sting of our bitter task. I miss your encouragement of my progress, and affirmations when I've done well. I miss the fact you're always right, and I miss that you weren't here to be right this time.

This war has grown so bitter in your absence. My dear friend, Talise, told me of such awful sadness I cannot hardly fathom. A war of reprisal has been going on since June in the lands of her kin, the five nations of the Iroquois allied to the British. Last year the Iroquois war parties attacked many Patriot settlers in the New York wilderness, burning and killing folks unable to protect themselves.

General Washington ordered Generals Sullivan and Clinton to wipe the Iroquois out. So far, they've burned over forty Iroquois villages, fields, gardens, and storehouses, leaving nothing left for the people of the Finger Lakes region. Talise fears they will be annihilated. Before the war, they were all one people; their blood is her blood, they all fought together in the French and Indian War. But this time they chose different sides. If they cannot find aid amongst the British, many of them will die of hunger and exposure in the coming months.

Henry tells me Washington aims to break the native alliance with the British, and these efforts will very likely succeed. The more difficult things get for the British, the sooner they will surrender. I understand it, in a strategic sense, and perhaps it was the only way, but I have long since left the notion that the suffering of war is only visited on those who fight it. This war touches everyone. There is no man, woman, or child whose life will not bear its scars, regardless of the color of their skin.

I have further confirmed that I am no nearer to being ready to be a mother. Last night, as we all sat around the fire, Abigail handed Mary-Beth to me after a feeding. She seemed content in my arms and even smiled. Her mood was so inviting that before long I found myself bouncing her on my knee, a thing she seemed very much to enjoy. After a few moments of this I lifted her into the air, cooing at her playfully. She put on a large grin, and everyone agreed she was delighted with my play. Then, all at once, her sweet face contorted into an awful grimace. Thinking she was going to cry, I opened my mouth to coo at her again, and that's when it happened. That sweet little angel of a girl puked in my mouth!

As you can imagine, I was quite shocked . . . it's not like I could have thrown her in disgust as I have many times with creatures and awful things the boys have brought me. Abigail gasped, Henry jumped from his stump, David stifled a laugh, and Abe—Abe burst out laughing. I just sat there, frozen in place as the sour milky substance contaminated my mouth, face and neck. At long last Henry lifted her from my arms, and Abigail broke me from my trance. I must have gargled water a dozen times and still I could taste it. Even now as I write about it, my saliva recreates the flavor in my mouth. The worst part is, I am fairly certain Mary-Beth was smiling at me all the while.

I awoke this morning with an ache in my head and body. Perhaps I spent too much of yesterday in the dreadful heat without drinking enough water; another reason I need you here, to remind me to care for myself. Mr. Musgrave, bless his soul, is too overwhelmed by what he doesn't know to notice the condition of his staff. He means well, but I believe he's missed his calling somewhere along the way.

Regrettably, fatigue and my pounding head is causing me to feel poorly. I pray you are well, and your work is not too burdensome. Take care of yourself, Tobias. If something were to happen to you, it would be more than my heart could bear.

Affectionately,

Mercy Young

"It's no good, Abigail," Mrs. Bell said. "Mercy's burning up, and that rash . . . you know what it is."

"The pox," Abigail gasped. "She was feeling poorly yesterday, but . . . not the pox, dear Lord, not the pox."

"We've had a handful of patients this month," Adelaide said. "Not an unusual number, but Mercy does tend to be a little more reckless in her comforting care."

"You and Mary-Beth shouldn't be near her," Mrs. Bell said. "It'd be the death of her."

Mercy groaned as their voices only aggravated the pounding in her head. It had come upon her so quickly, the aches, fever, and then the rash. She knew Mrs. Bell was right, the pox was almost certain death to an infant, and even as a young adult, her chances were not exceptional.

"Oh, my dear Mercy," Abigail sobbed. "You must fight it. With all your feisty spirit, you must fight it!"

"Out with you, now," Mrs. Bell chided. "The Good Lord will watch over her."

Mercy felt the wagon tremble as Abigail climbed out of the buckboard, her mother's muffled sobs faded into silence. She groaned again as her joints racked her with pain.

"I'm here, Mercy," Mrs. Bell said as softly as Mercy had ever heard her speak. "I'm right here. There aren't a more stubborn couple of ladies in all of the states. We're going to beat this."

Mercy felt a cool cloth dab at her forehead. Her thoughts were thick and foggy, and she couldn't remember what day it was.

"My letter?" Mercy mumbled.

"I sent it with Jonathan this morning," Mrs. Bell said, dabbing her again.

Mercy trembled as the cool rag had its effect.

"I'd give you a blanket, but you're burning up," Mrs. Bell said compassionately. "You're hot as a kettle."

"Henry?" Mercy asked.

"They're still off on one of their missions. We've heard no word, but you must stop your fretting and rest."

Her mind was a maze of hazy thoughts. She'd aided countless soldiers with the pox, some more fortunate than others. It was a cruel sickness, and the only cure seemed to be time itself. Some soldiers who'd survived had battled for the better part of a month before their fever broke. That wasn't the worst of it. The rash became raised bumps and blisters, distorting the flesh on faces and necks, hands and feet; some soldiers even went blind.

She tried not to think about it, tried not to worry, but she knew the truth of it. She knew the odds, she knew even if she survived, she may look like a gargoyle for the rest of her life. She shook with the thought of it. Reaching with her hand, she felt for the rash.

"No, Mercy . . ." Mrs. Bell chided, brushing her hand away.

"How bad?" Mercy whispered.

"It's mostly on your chest and neck at the moment, but if you touch it, it'll spread," Mrs. Bell said. "I had the pox once too, and there's hardly a mark on me. Now, rest."

The rash itched like a hundred mosquito bites. In the field hospital, they'd had to tie soldiers' hands to the cots if they wouldn't refrain from scratching. Some of them had gone mad...

She felt trapped between the aches and the itching, her trembling body and the sweat rolling off her forehead. It was maddening, but she felt too weak to fight it. Caught in the foggy exhaustion, she fell asleep.

***

"Mercy . . . Mercy," a voice called. "Come on girl, come back . . ."

As the darkness began to fade, pain met her from every joint and she let out a guttural groan.

"I know, girl, I know," Mrs. Bell chided. "But you must try and eat, or you'll have no strength for the fight. Come on now . . . come out of it."

Mercy struggled to open her eyes, her left cheek and forehead itched and burned from the rash, the irritating sensation ran down her back and up her arms, and she choked with the maddening helplessness of it. As she finally willed her eyes to open, she cried out as she could only see out of one of them.

"It's alright, it's alright," Mrs. Bell cooed, holding down her writhing body. "It's just some bandages over your blisters, your eye is fine."

Mercy stopped fighting, looking up at her through blurry tears.

"I know it's awful . . ." Mrs. Bell sighed. "But you've been out for the lion's share of two days. We must keep your strength up."

Mercy reached to wipe away her tears, but Mrs. Bell caught her hand and dabbed them away with a cloth. She felt terrible. Her stomach was both nauseous and gnawing at itself with hunger, she could feel every joint in her body resonating pain, and the rash that'd crept its way across her face burned and itched under her bandages. She felt like she was dying.

"I've got a little stew for you, with tender rabbit meat caught by your bird just this morning."

"Theo?"

"Yes, Adelaide and Benjamin took him on a walk in the woods. He's been frightful lonesome without you."

Mercy managed a weak smile.

Mrs. Bell reached over and helped Mercy sit up, it was an exhausting and painful effort, but they were able to get her into position so she wouldn't choke as she ate.

Mercy watched groggily as Mrs. Bell lifted a spoon from a bowl and blew on it gently. "Your fever is low at the moment, but it comes and goes with a fury."

Carefully she brought the spoon to Mercy's lips and tipped it, so the contents flowed into her mouth.

Mercy chewed slowly, but even that seemed tedious and painful, diluting her enjoyment of the stew's nourishing broth.

Mrs. Bell brought the spoon back to the bowl and repeated the process.

"Abigail?" Mercy asked.

Mrs. Bell smiled. "What can you expect? She's beside herself. Henry's nearly had to tie her to the wagon to keep her from coming to you. He's even threatened to send her back to Cambridge, though I don't think he's the kind of man who'd do such a thing."

Mercy managed another weak smile before the next bite. "Henry is back?" she asked.

"Yes, they had a successful battle at a place called Paulus Hook in New Jersey. Apparently, there was a British fort there they attacked in the wee hours of the morning; took them by surprise. They forded a canal in the dark and scurried up the embankment at the rear of the fort. Captured a hundred and fifty men and officers without hardly breaking a sweat."

As Mercy swallowed her third bite, her stomach turned, and Mrs. Bell scarcely had time to get her a pail before it all came back up.

"Lord, help us," Mrs. Bell prayed as she dabbed away the remnants at Mercy's mouth. "You are the Healer when nothing else will do. Please, grant us your healing mercies now . . ."

Chapter 13

Somewhere in the black, she was aware of a warm wet sensation, like that of a dog's tongue. It moved about her limbs rhythmically, and she decided to focus her aching mind on it, allowing it to pull her from the darkness. As she did, she became aware of sounds, drums in the distance, the dripping of water into a bowl, the laughter of a child somewhere nearby. Smells too entertained her senses, wood smoke, sweat, and . . . soap?

"Mama?" she groaned.

"Bless the Lord!" she heard a woman gasp. "No, girl, it's me . . . Mrs. Bell. Thank heavens, you've been out for days, so I thought to give you a bath."

Mercy's throat felt dry and sticky, and her joints still ached. She shivered as the water from Mrs. Bell's scrubbing evaporated from her skin.

"I'm almost finished," Mrs. Bell said. "Then we'll get you all covered back up."

"Water . . ." Mercy whispered.

There was a clanking of a ladle in a pail, and she felt Mrs. Bell gently tip her head so she could pour the water into her mouth.

Taking a sip, the water came too fast, causing her to choke, and Mrs. Bell withdrew the ladle, sitting her up to clear her lungs. The effort was painful and exhausting. After she'd recovered, Mrs. Bell tried again, this time with more success.

After a few swallows, Mrs. Bell laid her back down. Next, she tried to open her eyes, she strained with all her might, but her world remained dark. Reaching up, she tried to feel them, but Mrs. Bell pulled her hands back down. Panic seized her and she reached again, and again Mrs. Bell restrained her, the effort causing waves of pain to emanate from her joints.

"Am I . . . blind?" she choked.

There was a hesitation. "I don't know, Mercy. At the moment your eyes are swollen shut . . . perhaps for the best, to protect them from the rash."

Mercy stopped struggling.

"You're not but skin and bones . . . we must get some food into you," Mrs. Bell said.

Mercy tried to imagine her appearance, she'd delt with smallpox on many occasions. The blistering oozing rash was nauseating to behold, and the gaunt appearance of those poor souls racked with painful fevers filled her mind. She must look like death itself.

Mrs. Bell finished her bath, and gently placed a blanket over her. Mercy felt entirely trapped in her dark painful world. The feeling of claustrophobia and itchy agony was so maddening that, for a moment, she even despaired of life itself.

But then she heard something, mumbling voices through the wagon's canvas walls. Soft voices that carried her name. In her condition her senses were not keen, and she had trouble distinguishing who the mumblers may be, but her name . . . she knew her name. The mumbling was constant, first one voice, then another, and she was beginning to think she was going mad.

"Are there people outside?" she whispered.

"Yes," Mrs. Bell said. "Folks have been coming at all hours of the day to pray for you. Sometimes one or two at a time, other times a group of them. Soldiers, friends, your parents, Adelaide and Jonathan, your brothers, even Mr. Musgrave. Your friend, Talise, sent a peculiar native tea with Jonathan for when you're able, he's been looking after her in your stead. I doubt there is a soul in this camp you haven't left your mark on."

Hot tears forced their way out of her swollen eyes, rolled across her blotchy lumpy cheeks, and onto her sheets. She didn't want to let them down, all those people pulling for her, the voices on the other side of the canvas.

"That's right, Mercy. Keep fighting, girl," Mrs. Bell said, laying a hand on her shoulder.

———❦———

Light. It was the first measure of hope she'd had in days. The swelling in her eyes must have reduced as she was able to open them in fine slits. The opening was so slight, all she could make out was the light itself, but it was something.

The next thing she noticed was taste; the broth Mrs. Bell carefully spooned into her mouth tasted divine, and that's when it hit her . . . she had an appetite.

"Slowly, slowly, Mercy . . ." Mrs. Bell chided. "I don't fancy you spittin' it up all over me due to your haste. Your fever broke this morning, you'd best believe we'll be inundated with visitors once the word gets out. You still have quite the rash, and we need to get your strength up to keep the fever at bay . . ." She paused. "You gave me quite a scare," Mrs. Bell choked, patting Mercy's arm.

Mercy swallowed the broth in her mouth. "Thank you for nursing me."

"I just knew you'd pull through," Mrs. Bell said, swallowing hard. "Certainly, Mercy Young would pull through."

Mercy swallowed another spoonful.

"You have a letter here from Captain Davis . . . Would you like me to read it to you?"

Mercy nodded.

Papers crinkled and Mrs. Bell began.

"August 30, 1779. My Dear Mercy, I pray you will forgive me for the brevity of this letter. I only just received Abigail's letter telling me of your condition and I was compelled by heart and mind to send a return immediately. You must know that my thoughts and prayers are and ever will be of you. You are strong, Mercy Young, and I am extremely confident that by God's grace, you will recover. As you well know, I am always right when it comes to matters of combat, and of this I am sure; you will prevail."

Mercy chuffed. "Always right . . ."

She felt Mrs. Bell place the back of her hand on her forehead. "Are you alright, Mercy? Suddenly you look flushed."

"As well as can be expected," Mercy replied, hiding a smile.

"Right . . ." Mrs. Bell sighed. "I would like to be cross with you . . ." She turned back to the letter.

"I very well know your reckless behavior towards patients with the pox and fever, but that is your way, and God only knows the number of souls we've retained because of your brash practices. I have no doubt the miseries and trials you now suffer will only strengthen your resolve to be a compassionate angel of mercy to whomever the Good Lord should lay in your care, even if such a person were to have leprosy."

Again, Mercy found herself smiling.

"I requested leave to come tend to you personally, but it seems we shall be seeing strong action soon and my services will be vital here. I thought our departure was the most difficult test the cause would place on me, but now, knowing you are in such a state, I find myself pondering the merits of desertion."

Mercy placed her hands over her mouth to hide her joyful smile. She could feel Mrs. Bell watching her.

"It's alright, Mercy," Mrs. Bell sighed. "The doctor delivers good medicine even from afar. A merry heart *is* good medicine after all."

Mercy nodded but didn't lower her hands.

"Though I don't believe getting shot would do either the cause or yourself any benefit," Mrs. Bell continued. "I'm afraid that I must ask you to fight this noble battle without me, albeit for me. You are the first light of dawn; rays of hope at the end of a long and difficult night. I look for you, there, at the end of all this, and my heart finds strength to keep on. You must prevail, Mercy, my dear friend. You must keep shining, there, at the horizon, for me. Faithfully yours, Tobias Davis."

Mercy's eyes filled with tears and Mrs. Bell pulled her into her arms.

"He's an average doctor," Mrs. Bell sniffled. "But he's awfully good with a quill."

Both of them chuckled.

"I can see why you're fond of him, Mercy," Mrs. Bell said, folding the letter and placing it in Mercy's hand.

Mercy held the letter tightly in her fingers as Mrs. Bell helped her lie back down. How blessed she was to have so many people pulling for her. Many of the boys she'd tended to had only had her. It was an awfully despairing sickness to go through alone. She thanked the Lord for her family and friends, for bringing her this far through yet another storm.

During the week that followed, Mercy continued to recover. The swelling around her eyes lessoned and the rash retreated. Everyone praised God when her eyesight fully returned. She was thin and frail now, and still a sickly pale. The rash had a while to heal yet, and the scabs fall off, before she'd be able to mingle with folks again. Still, she was allowed up and out of the wagon for a little while each day, though she was not permitted to enter areas frequented by others.

Henry, who'd already had the pox, came and sat with her as often as he could. Telling her of the goings on in camp, the mischief of David and Nathaniel Bell, and bringing Abigail's love. She could tell her condition worried him, he tried to hide it, but his kind sad eyes betrayed him. He wasn't good at watching his loved ones suffer, especially when there was nothing he could do about it.

"Abigail's worried sick about you," Henry said. "She's already gone and replaced your wardrobe as everything will have to be burned. She prays for you without hardly taking a meal or rest. For a woman who appeared to be barren, she's earned her strips as a mother."

"She has," Mercy agreed. "I feel dreadful so much of it is on my account."

"As you should," Henry jested.

Mercy smiled.

"No, I think she'd gladly say that it's far better to have children who cause you to worry, than to have no children to worry about."

"I'm sure you cause her much worry as well," Mercy said.

"That's just being a good husband," Henry replied. "It's our duty to do all manner of reckless foolishness, what else would our wives talk about amongst themselves if we didn't? The weather? Harvest? A new calf perhaps? No, these dull topics are reserved for their husbands. Wives . . . they need something a little more . . . dramatic." Henry smiled.

Mercy thought about it for a moment and had to agree. Most of the women she knew wouldn't talk about anything unless it got them all flustered. Men, on the other hand, could muse for a morning over the color of the dirt in their field, or the best way to stack firewood for drying.

"Still," Mercy said. "You'd best not tell her that."

"Never," Henry winked.

Chapter 14

Smoke rose lazily from the heap of smoldering fabric that comprised Mercy's wardrobe and bedding over the past month. Her rash had dried up and the scabs had fallen off, leaving behind a few small scars hardly noticeable unless one knew where to look. Her frame was thin, and she tired easily, but her appetite and strength were returning day by day.

The wagon was stripped to the frame, everything was either scrubbed with a vengeance or burned. Mrs. Bell had assured everyone that Mercy was indeed over the disease and Abigail had been the first to swallow her in a tearful embrace, lifting her feet off the ground.

That first afternoon of freedom, David, Mable, and Nathaniel offered to take Mercy on an adventure to celebrate. Theo felt heavy on her shoulder as they went, but she was glad to have her friend so close once more. The day was warm, but not sweltering like it had been, and here and there nuts could be heard falling in the forest.

The seasons were changing, summer was giving way to fall. Soon, the forest would be painted in radiant yellows, reds, and oranges. The harvests would come in from the fields, and folks would celebrate the bounty of their labors. There would be parties, cider, and music. And for a moment, folks would forget about their troubles, about the war, about the coming winter. For a moment, everything would seem . . . right.

Mercy smiled as she rested on a log, her body not yet able to carry her like it used to. David was busy playing an Iroquois warrior, trying to get his hands on Mable while Nathaniel loaded his stick musket as quickly as his hands could move and returned fire in her defense. Theo dismounted and took up a position beside Mercy on the log, leaning into her fingers as she stroked his tufted head.

The sun's rays poured through the leaves of the forest canopy warming her body and soul. She was alive again. She closed her eyes, listening to the stream rolling over pebbles behind her as birds called to one another in the trees around them, her senses glad to be of service once more.

"That's not fair!" Nathaniel exclaimed, drawing Mercy out of her serenity. "I shot you three times!"

"No, you didn't!" David retorted. "I was moving too fast!"

"Too fast?!" Nathaniel balked. "I've seen slugs move faster!"

"Ha! Is that so?! Maybe we should have a race, then we'll see who the *real* slug is!" David replied.

David was a couple inches shorter than Nathaniel, but he was lean and fast. Nathaniel, being a Bell, was of a stockier build, and heavy on his feet. David could beat him in a foot race, but in a fist fight Nathaniel would have all the advantages.

"You might be faster than me, Dave, but you're not as fast as a musket ball," Nathaniel countered.

Mable wandered over and took a seat next to Mercy while the boys sorted it out.

"I know that, but even my papa, who's a marksman, says he doesn't shoot at a moving target cause they're too hard to hit, and I was moving fast," David replied.

"I shot you when you were hiding behind that tree," Nathaniel said, pointing to a chestnut.

"You couldn't see me!"

"Yes, I could! Ask Mable!"

The boys both looked at her expectantly.

Mable fidgeted for a moment. "Well, I couldn't see all of you," she began. "Only your backside."

"You shot me in the backside?!" David gasped. "That's dishonorable!"

"I've tended to more than a handful who'd been shot in their backsides, Dave," Mercy added.

"It's war," Nathaniel said. "Sometimes you've got to take what the enemy gives ya."

David placed his hand on his rump. "The indignity," he said, placing the back of his hand on his forehead and falling dramatically to the ground.

"Looks like I'm saved," Mable said.

"Looks like." Mercy smiled.

"Okay, let's do it again!" David said, hopping up from the ground.

Mable chuffed, pushing herself up from the log. Holding out her hand she helped lift Mercy, and they were off again down the trail with David flanking them through the undergrowth.

"I'm glad you made it," Mable said.

"Me too," Mercy said. "Your mama wouldn't let me quit. It got pretty dark, Mable. There were days . . . when I couldn't see, couldn't feel anything but pain and the unrelenting itch, feeling like I was going mad. I wanted to die . . . but your mama wouldn't give up on me. Some nights she'd stay up and rock me, humming hymns, keeping the voices in my head at bay, giving me peace when it didn't seem possible. She was the one who was strong, Mable. The devil couldn't have me . . . not while your mama was standing guard."

"My papa used to say she was a lioness," Mable smiled. "But that's usually when they were having a quarrel."

"I wouldn't be here if she wasn't," Mercy said. "She's another hero in my story."

"I'm sorry, Mable," Nathaniel gasped, falling to the ground beside them.

"Spoils of war!" David cried, leaping onto the trail and starting for Mable.

Stooping over, Mercy picked up Nathaniel's stick and pretended to shoot David.

"What?!" David balked. "Girls don't shoot!"

"This girl does," Mercy smiled.

Swallowing his pride for her sake, David gripped his chest and fell over.

"My hero," Mable swooned.

"It was nothing," Mercy said, leaning on the stick to steady herself, her head still spinning from the rapid motion.

"Are you alright?" Mable asked.

"Yeah, just tired."

"Maybe we should get you back."

"Awe," David groaned, picking himself up off the ground. "But I haven't even captured Mable and made her my squaw yet."

"You'll get me next time," Mable said.

Mercy lifted Theo to her shoulder, and they were off.

A couple of days later, Mercy rose out of bed feeling better than she had in weeks. The sun was already up warming the canvas, and she had to admit she was growing rather accustomed to sleeping in. Pulling on her dress, she stepped through the flap and out onto the buckboard. It was a beautiful morning.

"Good morning," Abigail said as she worked some laundry in a basin near the fire with Mary-Beth crawling about the grass a few feet away.

"Good morning, Mama."

"You have your color back," Abigail smiled. "I saved you a bit of bacon and an egg for breakfast if you're up to it."

Mercy climbed down out of the wagon and fetched the frypan off the side. She felt like she could eat several eggs, but knew it was best to take it slow.

"Henry and Benjamin were called to arms early this morning. Apparently, there was an incident with some Tories that needed sorting."

"I don't know how we'll all learn to see eye to eye when this is over," Mercy said. "There's going to be a lot of bad blood."

"Aye, the Good Lord will have His work cut out for Him."

In a few minutes the sound of bacon in the pan had Mercy's stomach churning. The smell was so delicious, she began to salivate. Cracking the egg, she added it to the pan and watched as the clear liquid around the yolk began to whiten.

Suddenly, she felt a tugging on her dress and looked down to see Mary-Beth trying to pull herself up beside her.

"She knows the sound of eggs," Abigail mused. "I've been slipping her bits of mine now that her teeth are starting to show."

Mercy carefully removed the pan from the fire and placed the bacon and egg on a plate. After saying grace, she tore into it like a starving man.

"Slow down, Mercy," Abigail chided. "It's not like the food is going anywhere."

Mercy did slow down, a little. She was nearing the end of the egg when Mary-Beth pulled on her dress again, cooing expectantly.

"I suppose," Mercy said. "But you'd better be grateful."

Picking up a bit of egg, she held it to the baby's mouth. Mary-Beth opened wide, and Mercy dropped it inside.

"She's like your owl," Abigail said. "Now that you've fed her, you'll never be rid of her."

"Awweee, that's okay," Mercy said, lifting her sister in her arms. "Isn't it?"

Mary-Beth smiled and cooed.

As Mercy bounced her gently on her knee, she saw Jonathan Bell approaching. He'd been faithful in helping Mrs. Bell care for her, and Mercy hadn't gotten the opportunity to thank him.

"It's good to see you up and in fine spirits," Jonathan said when he arrived.

"I have you and your mother to thank for that," Mercy said.

"I was about to go and do a few chores for Talise. I thought, maybe, you'd like to join me?" he asked.

"A little walking would probably do me some good," Mercy said.

"Good, I'll be leaving just as soon as I collect my axe."

"Leave your plate, I'll wash it for you," Abigail said.

"Thanks, Mama."

Jonathan held a branch up out of her way as they navigated the narrow trail leading to the clearing and Talise's longhouse. He'd been a constant over the past month, taking time to check on her, and making sure Talise and her family were looked after. She'd been wrong about him, he was simple and perhaps at times naïve of the feelings of others due to his strict pious upbringing, but underneath it all, she'd discovered a sincere and adventurous spirit she'd grown quite fond of.

"Thank you," she said.

"Talise will be delighted to see you," he said. "Her concern for you was constant."

"Thank you for looking after them; it would've been difficult to prepare for winter without your help."

"I—" he sighed. "At first, my motives were simply to hear you say that. I've been so desperate for a way to garner your affections."

She looked up at him, but his face was set straight ahead, and he made no effort to meet her gaze. She was aware of the efforts he'd made, both to rise and meet her expectations, and also to win her affection.

"I'm a little embarrassed, but I have no one else in whom to confide . . . and I feel a little awkward saying such, as you are my only confidant," he continued. "But I feel as though something unexpected has happened, and I'm not rightly sure what it is I feel."

Mercy braced herself for what he was about to say.

"Though I began earnestly seeking your affections, I feel as though my own have wandered." He paused, thinking carefully. "I find myself longing to come back to this clearing from the moment I leave it. This family . . . they've become as dear to me as my own."

Mercy's ears tingled, and her pulse quickened as she processed his words.

He stopped just before the clearing, finally looking down on her with warm eyes, before holding back one last branch and stepping out into the clearing.

"Jonathan!" Okwaho shouted, catching sight of him.

The little boy raced across the clearing with his sister toddling behind him. As they drew near, Jonathan dropped to a knee and scooped Okwaho up in one arm. Careful of the axe, he lifted Kaniehtiio up in the other. Standing, he carried them back towards the longhouse where Talise had stepped to the doorway.

Mercy waved as they crossed the clearing, and Talise set off to meet them. She felt warm walking behind him, watching Okwaho wrap his arms around Jonathan's neck. It felt . . . right. Like this Jonathan had been trapped inside the Jonathan she'd first met and was just looking for an opportunity to escape. This Jonathan *could* possibly win her affections . . . but looking at Okwaho and Kaniehtiio in his arms she knew they'd already captured his.

"I heard you were near to death," Talise said, taking her by the hands. "Thank the Lord for your strong spirit."

"It was pretty awful," Mercy said. "It's good to be able to move about again, I was losing my wits cooped up in that wagon all day."

"We were just about to head to the stream to catch some fish. Would you like to learn how to catch fish the Oneida way?" Talise asked.

"Oh yes, please," Mercy answered.

Jonathan dropped his axe at the woodpile and helped Talise gather a couple of fish baskets and a cone-shaped apparatus that was as tall as Mercy. It was made of reeds and canes loosely woven together, the mouth of the cone was open, an arm's-width across, and it tapered down to a point.

"We're not bringing any fishing canes?" Mercy asked.

"No, this fish trap is all we need," Talise said.

Chapter 15

When they reached the stream, Talise studied it, leading the five of them along the edge until she found what she was looking for.

"See how this deep pool rises gradually to a shallow end where the water only reaches halfway to the knee?"

Mercy nodded.

"This is the perfect place to lay our trap."

Jonathan set down the trap, and Mercy and Talise set down their baskets.

"We're going to take stones and make a V shape here at the shallow end, leaving just enough space to place our trap in the middle," Talise said, kicking off her moccasins.

Jonathan shrugged at Mercy and began removing his shoes and stockings and Mercy did the same. The water was cold on her skin, but the sensation of doing something adventurous again was heavenly. Together they splashed about the shallows, collecting stones to create the V. Every now and again a crayfish would shoot out from under a stone and Okwaho would set off after it.

When the V was complete, Talise set the trap at its center, so the end product looked very much like a funnel.

"Now comes the fun part," Talise said. "We'll go upstream until the water gets shallow again, form a line all the way across it, and splash our way all the way back to the trap!"

Mercy's eyes widened. The stream must have been at least waist deep in the pool . . . Abigail was sure to have a fit when she returned to camp sopping wet, especially after recovering from the pox only a short while ago. Still, it did look like a lot of fun, and she really wanted to see how the trap worked. Bunching up her dress, she lifted it above her knees, determined to make the best of it.

Jonathan put Kaniehtiio on his shoulders and held onto Okwaho's hand as they started into the stream. When their line had been formed shoulder to shoulder, they began stomping and splashing their way towards the trap. Okwaho began laughing instantly as Jonathan's large stomps sent water spraying all over him. Kaniehtiio joined her brother in squealing with delight at the spectacle as the four of them continued their charge.

Mercy could feel her dress growing heavy as the water deepened; it was hopeless. She looked over at Talise who carried her sopping hem as she continued stomping, seemingly unphased by it. Shrugging her shoulders, she determined not to worry about it and continued on with increased splashing fervor.

By the time the five of them stumbled their way to the trap, they were all soaked from head to toe and laughing uncontrollably.

"Quick, lift it, lift it!" Talise called.

Jonathan charged forward and lifted the mouth of the trap out of the water. To Mercy's surprise, a half dozen trout were caught fast at the narrow end of the trap.

"It's like swimming and fishing at the same time," Mercy panted.

Jonathan studied the fish in the trap. "It's incredible. Catching fish without a net or a hook. Everything about it, made from the forest and reeds."

"I can teach you how to make one," Talise offered.

"I'd love to learn," Jonathan said, handing her the trap so she could empty it in her basket.

"Now what?" Mercy asked.

"Now, we do it again," Talise smiled.

"Do it again! Do it again!" Okwaho chanted.

Mercy wrung out her dress and the five of them headed back upstream.

By the end of the afternoon, Mercy was thoroughly worn out, her feet ached from stumbling over stones under the water, but her heart was full. Together they'd managed to catch twenty-three fish, laugh until their sides hurt, and learn more about each other. Mercy had spent an hour spinning slowly beside Talise's fire in hopes of softening Abigail's berating back at camp.

When they could linger no longer, they said their goodbyes and set off on the trail through the woods once again.

"I can see what you mean," Mercy said as they walked. "You really do fit there."

Jonathan scoffed. "My mother would tan my hide like a child's if she knew I was even entertaining such a notion. I can hardly believe it myself; I've never thought of her people as anything but heathens and savages. I'm ashamed of myself . . . if they knew . . ."

"That was your ignorance talking back then, but it's not who you are now," Mercy said. "None of us can change who we were, but we can change who we are. Aren't the Lord's mercies new every morning?"

Jonathan nodded.

"Don't be so sure about your mama . . . Every time I have been, I've been wrong," Mercy admitted. "She really just wants what's best for all of us . . . even if she may be wrong sometimes about what exactly that might be."

"It's madness though, right?" Jonathan said. "Her husband died only a short while ago, she already had a family . . . and I'm a Puritan, a shoemaker—I don't know anything about living in the wild."

"You're learning fast, and her heart is on the mend. It's obvious she enjoys your company. Just keep being yourself, and take things a day at a time," Mercy said. "These things have a way of working themselves out."

"Who told you that?" he scoffed.

"My mama," Mercy smiled. "When we were talking about you."

Jonathan scoffed again.

"Mercy Josephine Young!" Abigail gasped once they reached the wagons.

"I'll uhh, see you later." Jonathan bowed before setting off for the Bell's, leaving Mercy alone.

"What has gotten into you?! Are you daft, girl? You're not but skin and bones and you want to go and catch a fever again?"

"I'm sorry, Mama," Mercy said. "But it couldn't be helped."

"I don't want to hear it! Get up in that wagon this instant and take that dress off! I'll get some broth warming."

Mercy climbed into the wagon as she was told.

"Lord, have mercy . . ." Abigail muttered as she prepared the broth outside. "Haven't any of my children got any sense?"

Mercy smiled to herself. Abigail was all bark and no bite. She'd probably spend the remainder of the evening waiting on Mercy hand and foot, scolding her all the while.

When she emerged from the wagon, Abigail threw a wool blanket around her shoulders and ushered her over to the fire.

"Are you trying to break your mama's heart, Mercy? I nearly lost you; don't you understand that? You haven't even gotten your strength back, and you're already running around the woods like a wild animal?"

"I'm sorry, Mama. Talise needed our help catching some fish."

"What? With your bare hands? Go swimming after 'em, did you?!"

"No, we used a fish trap."

"I don't care what it was, Mercy . . . you can't be careless with your health," Abigail said, lifting a spoonful of broth to her mouth. "The Good Lord didn't rescue you just so you could go charging right back into the fire."

"I know," Mercy said, swallowing another spoonful. "I won't let it happen again."

"Ha!" Abigail scoffed. "Don't make promises you can't keep, Mercy."

Mercy smiled. "I love you, Mama."

"Ohhh, there you go, buttering me up," Abigail smiled, kissing her on the forehead. "And I love you too. Though I refuse to let your flattery have its way with me when I'm cross!"

"What happened to Mercy?" David piped up.

"She decided to go for a swim," Abigail said.

"In her dress?!" David asked, eyeing it hanging from a wagon wheel. "Boy, Mercy, that fever must have really messed with your head."

"Indeed," Abigail mused.

"It won't happen again," Mercy mumbled.

Three days later, Henry, Benjamin, and Abe returned from their hunt for the mischievous Tories. Mercy was glad to have them all home without a scratch once more. Abigail prepared a breakfast of ham and eggs, and the family sat around the fire sipping coffee.

"They let me march with the men, Mercy," Abe said. "I'm not carrying a musket yet, but I get to come along."

"That's more adventuring than I'm allowed to do," Mercy replied. "I can't even go for a swim."

Abigail scoffed.

"Did you see any Tories, Abe?" David asked.

"We didn't find any."

"It's difficult when they can simply melt back into regular society," Henry said, taking a puff on his pipe. "The local militia has been called up to keep them at bay."

"Any word on the war in the South?" Mercy asked.

"Yes, big news. A combined army of French and Continentals began a siege of Savannah on the sixteenth. If they're able to capture the port, the British will have to expend more resources to find another port city to supply their southern campaign."

"About time the French got their hands dirty," Abigail said.

"It's a step," Henry agreed.

"I wonder what Captain Davis would say about it?" Mercy said.

"Come on, Mercy," Abe said. "It's two armies against one."

"I wish it were that simple," Henry said.

"*That* sounds like something Captain Davis would say," Abigail said.

"Unfortunately, it's the truth," Henry said. "And without the French navy, even if they're able to retake the port, the redcoats will simply load their soldiers up on ships and land them somewhere else."

"Meanwhile, their navy continues to raid our ports, driving up the cost of supplies, food, and munitions," Ben said.

"Aye," Henry agreed. "The war is getting expensive for everyone. It's going to come down to who breaks first."

"Why doesn't Congress just give the army more stuff?" David asked.

"The government doesn't actually possess its own supplies, or money, for that matter. It takes it from the people and distributes it wherever it believes it's needed, and not always for the better," Henry said. "That's what levees and taxes are: a burden placed on the people to pay for the government's projects."

"I thought that's why we were fighting the king in the first place," Mercy said.

"It was high taxes coupled with a lack of representation that lit the fuse," Henry said. "Then the king moved to disarm the colonists for fear of revolt, and that set everything off. We believe people should have the right to be involved in the processes that determine how our government taxes us, and on what it is spent. We also believe that every citizen has the right to defend themselves, and to be amply armed to do so, even if the party they need protection from is the government itself."

"That's why Papa was on the green," Ben said. "The king was coming for our munitions so the colonies wouldn't be able to rise up against his oppression, and that's not the world he wanted us to grow up in."

David looked at his feet. "I'm beginning to forget what he was like."

Abigail put an arm around him and pulled him in close. "I haven't," she said. "Though I've never met him, I see him in every one of you."

"Aye," Henry agreed. "A father couldn't be prouder than to have the four of you as his legacy."

Mercy smiled to herself. Her papa would be proud of them, and he'd rest easy seeing the love and care with which Henry and Abigail took up his mantle. Through all of it, the Good Lord had been faithful.

Chapter 16

September 30, 1779

My dear Mercy,

I am relieved beyond the quill's ability to tell it that you are once again well. Though your condition caused me worry, I had no doubt your stubborn character would be sure to get the final word; that has always been my experience. Your recovery is a blessing to my patients as well, as my mind will not be so divided with worry for you. I long for my home among you all with every ounce of my lonely heart. You must make every effort to keep well and abide by Abigail's instructions.

It will probably seem humorous that some part of my consciousness still anticipates seeing your owl every time I embark from my quarters, eyeing me incredulously as though I were keeping you from him. Every frog's croak reminds me of our adventures with your brothers. Your laughter and smile at my faltering in the river is acted out again and again like a play in my mind.

It is an odd sensation, when these memories come, I find myself both comforted and feeling all the more alone.

The siege of Savannah goes on with little gained. It is a peculiar thing, British, Germans, French, Continentals, and militias, and the most peculiar thing of all, African slaves—fighting on either side with the promise of earning their freedom at the end of their service—men drawn from their homes, near and far, to participate in this conflict, of whom many will never return.

The British have scuttled their ships in the mouth of the channel, a clever strategy, preventing the newly-returned French fleet from rendering aid in the bombardment of the city's fortifications. The redcoats hold strong positions, and I fear to take them will be costly. Even with the world against them, the king's men continue to conduct themselves shrewdly and professionally, though I loathe to admit it.

As soldiers continue to fall, I find myself asking the question; what drives a man to long for an empire? What is it that makes him want to tread another person under his shoe? It is one thing to hunger for adventure, to see new lands and the beauty thereof, but where does the need to own another's world come from? The men who dig the trenches, man the guns, and charge the ramparts will receive only crumbs in comparison to those who sit on padded thrones. And kings will receive glory for blood they never spilled on battlefields they never beheld. It is, all of it, madness.

I pray over the battles that lie ahead. May our boys be swift and courageous, our enemies stumble in their pride, and may our ever-faithful Creator make a way for us to be together again.

Your faithful friend,
Tobias Davis

"He sounds as lonely as Job," Abigail sighed. "You're probably the only person on this earth who's ever known his feelings. I pray you are not careless with them."

"Mama, you make me out to be as cold and heartless a person as King George!"

"A man's heart is not something to be handled lightly, is all I'm saying. Especially the heart of a good man. I doubt there are many things more precious or tender, which is why they hide it away under so many layers of strength and resolve. It's a rare thing, to know a man's heart, and few are the women who ever truly have."

"Then you must be a lucky woman," Mercy said, nudging her.

"Luck has nothing to do with it . . . I've been a faithful and sure harbor these many years. For all his adventuresome spirit, what a man truly longs for is peace from his storms. If you can become that place, that harbor, you'll get to know the man who no one else gets to see."

"You're fond of Captain Davis, aren't you?"

"He reminds me of Henry, and if given the choice, I'd choose Henry over General Washington himself."

"As would I," Mercy agreed.

"He's a good man, Mercy. Take great care with his heart, as he seems to have entrusted it to you."

"I know he is . . . and he's a good friend. I just . . . my heart's not sure I'm cut out to be anyone's harbor just yet. Everyone tells me I'm a woman, that courtship is the next step, but I still feel very much like a girl."

"And that's alright, Mercy. Your heart will let you know when it's ready. Everyone's journey is different, we all arrive at different times, but that's what makes them all special."

"Were you sure?"

"Absolutely, and I'm glad that I waited until I was."

"Weren't you worried?"

"About what, dear?"

"Well, marriage is for the rest of your life. What if, what if everything changed and you couldn't do the things you used to? What if Henry chose a life that didn't suit you? What if—"

"You're forgetting, Mercy. I knew him, I saw who he was under all the layers. And the Good Lord is the one who gave me peace. By the time we were wed, I was sure. The Lord's book tells us that perfect love casts out fear . . . When you know it, in here," she said, placing her hand over her heart. "You will have the peace you're looking for. The Lord knows His timing; have faith and wait for it."

"Yes, Mama," Mercy answered.

"Now, let's get these breakfast dishes finished, and then . . ." she said looking around. "I'd like you to take me fishing."

"You want to go fishing?!"

"You seem to enjoy it . . . and I enjoy eating fresh fish. Besides you'll be back working with Mr. Musgrave and Adelaide soon, now that your strength's returning," Abigail said sheepishly.

"I'd *love* to go fishing with you, Mama," Mercy said, scrubbing the dish in her hand with a little more zeal.

After they'd finished the dishes, Mercy collected a couple of canes they'd been using over the summer while Abigail left Mary-Beth in Mable's care, and they set off for the stream. The leaves were changing now, though only a few were falling—harbingers of the winter ahead.

When they reached the stream, Mercy studied it. She wanted to find the perfect spot where Abigail was sure to have success. She wandered upstream for a bit until she found a small deep pool; looking beneath the ripples, she could see the dark silhouettes of fish darting here and there.

"I think this is the spot," she said. "I'll roll a couple of logs and find us some worms, and you can unravel the twine on the canes. Be careful of the hooks though."

Setting off into the woods, Mercy found a couple of manageable logs, not so rotten they'd fall apart when she tried to roll them, but rotten enough to have been there a while. Bracing herself against the first, she dug her toes into the soft earth and pushed with all her might. To her relief, it rolled over rather easily, and underneath were a half-dozen plump worms.

Pouncing on the worms quickly, she managed to come away with four and a half. Satisfied there were enough worms to get started, she made her way back to the stream with Theo dancing delightedly on her shoulder.

"I found us a few worms," Mercy said, setting four of them down and sliding the half worm onto Abigail's hook.

"Poor dear," Abigail said.

"You don't even like bugs," Mercy said, scrunching up her forehead.

"I know, but it does seem a pitiful way to go."

"Only if we don't catch a fish," Mercy said. "Here, lift your cane up like this, and then swing the line out into the slow-moving water of that pool."

Abigail did as she was told.

"Perfect," Mercy smiled. "Now, just wait until your cork goes under and then jerk your cane up quickly to set the hook."

Mercy turned her back to the stream while she worked on threading her own worm onto the hook.

"Oh, goodness, Mercy. My cork has disappeared!" Abigail squawked.

Mercy turned to see Abigail's line stretched taut to where her cork had disappeared under the ripples.

"Set the hook! Set the hook!" Mercy coached.

Abigail jerked her cane upward with such excited force, the small fish came blasting out of the water, flying right at her. Shrieking, she dropped her cane and leapt out of the way just as the fish passed by where she'd been standing. Hitting the end of Abigail's line, the hook became dislodged, and the fish skittered across the pebbles, flopping this way and that.

Without instruction or invitation, Theo exploded from Mercy's shoulder and landed beside the fish. Flicking it into the air with his beak, he caught it and swallowed it in one swift motion.

Abigail stood gasping with her hand on her chest, watching the whole spectacle. Then, a smile tugged at the corners of her mouth, and she burst out laughing.

Mercy breathed a sigh of relief and began to laugh along with her.

Catching her breath, Abigail said, "It looks like I may have overdone it. Still, it's rather rude of your bird to steal my first fish," she said in feigned offense.

"I'm sorry, Mama, he's been spoiled," Mercy confessed.

"It's no matter," Abigail said, waving her hand. "That was exciting! I'd like to try it again."

After getting her line straightened out, Mercy rebaited her hook and Abigail tossed it back out into the stream. Mercy's cork had only just hit the water when Abigail's disappeared again. This time, Abigail set the hook with a little more finesse and her cane bent over as the fish realized its plight.

"Oh dear, Mercy, it's going to tug the cane from my hands, what do I do?"

"We have to wait—" Then Mercy's cork went under, and she set the hook. "I have one too!"

Mercy looked over as Abigail's cane was pulled back and forth while her mama held on for dear life, her eyes wide with excitement.

"We have to wear them down a bit," Mercy coached. "Mine's not so big, I'll land it, and then help with yours."

Backing up from the shore, Mercy drew a moderate trout out of the water where it flopped frantically. Once again Theo opened his wings."

"No, Theo, this one's ours," Mercy chided, reaching up and catching him by the foot.

Ruffling his feathers in frustration, Theo settled on her shoulder. Arriving at the fish, Mercy unhooked it and placed it in a basket.

"Oh no, you don't," Abigail scolded the fish on her line as she lifted her cane in opposition to the fish's tugging.

"It seems to be wearing down, start walking back from the bank, it'll bring him to shore where we can land him."

Abigail obeyed and in a few moments a fish slightly larger than Mercy's was flopping on the pebbles. Unhooking it, Mercy picked it up and held it for Abigail to see.

"My, it is a beautiful creature—for a fish, that is," Abigail smiled.

"Do you want to hold it?" Mercy asked.

"I doubt I've ever held a *live* fish before," Abigail said, holding out her hands.

Gently placing the fish in Abigail's hands, Mercy let go.

"It makes me nervous," Abigail said, holding the fish with a bit of trepidation. "Like it could start flopping at any moment."

As if on command, the fish flopped hard and squirted right out of Abigail's hands and onto the pebbles below.

"Get it, Mercy!" Abigail cheered as Mercy attempted to pounce on the fish as it flopped ever closer to the water's edge.

Twice Mercy had the fish in her hands only to have it squirt out again. Abigail squealed and cheered as the fish hit the water, but Mercy was fast enough to scoop it back onto the shore where it continued to flop. At last, covered in sand and debris, Mercy was able to secure the fish and get it into the basket when they noticed that Mercy's fish was nowhere to be found, and neither was Theo.

"Argh! Theo!" Mercy said, shaking her fist in the air.

"I guess it's been a while since you've been fishing," Abigail said. "Poor creature had a hard time of it while you were sick. Had to catch food on his own and live off of scraps."

"Yeah . . . *poor* creature," Mercy said, rolling her eyes.

"Well, that just means we need to catch a few more," Abigail smiled. "Would you mind doing the worm part?" she winced.

"Sure," Mercy replied.

By the time they headed back for camp, they had a dozen nice trout in the basket and Theo had returned looking as innocent as ever. Mercy couldn't stay angry with him though, it was the most she'd heard Abigail laugh in over a year, and that was a sound she cherished. Abigail was the best of mamas; she deserved an afternoon of joy.

"I can see why you like it," Abigail said. "There's a mystery to it, and excitement, the anticipation kept me on edge the entire time . . . I can feel the strain in my back! When the men get back from their foraging, they'll be elated to have fried fish for dinner."

Chapter 17

"Are you *sure* you have to begin back at the hospital today?" Abigail pleaded. "It's your birthday, after all."

"Yes," Mercy said, giving her a peck on the cheek. "Adelaide just came for me, there was a cannon burst and a dozen boys were injured. It's too many for them to handle on their own. I'm feeling as good as new, and the work will be good for me."

"They're lucky to have you," Abigail said. "Have someone fetch me if you need an extra hand. Mrs. Bell can watch Mary-Beth if necessary."

"I will," Mercy said, setting off towards the field hospital.

She felt excited, which was strange considering the mournful work that was hers, but to be a part of it all again . . . she'd missed it. Arriving at the hospital, she stepped inside and donned a clean apron.

"Oh, Mercy," Mr. Musgrave called over his patient. "It's good to have you back. I pray you haven't forgotten how to care for the wounded."

"No, sir," Mercy said, stepping up to a cot with a wounded soldier lying on it.

Adelaide gave her a quick appreciative smile before returning to her own patient. Looking down on the soldier in front of her, Mercy could see a moist crimson stain on his left upper arm, and another on his left thigh. His face was pocked with scratches and some of his hair had been singed. Pulling out a pair of scissors, she cut the man's sleeve off and opened the hole in his breeches in order to determine which wound was the greater threat.

Thankfully, neither wound spurted, and she elected to tend to his thigh first. After giving the man a little ale, she assured him she'd do her best, but it was going to hurt. Taking the forceps, she spread the wound open with her left hand. The man moaned, and all the emotions and anxiety she'd recovered from while being sick came flooding back.

Taking a deep breath, she forced her own feelings back down and gently guided the forceps into the wound, searching for the bit of iron which had created it. The man lunged for her, forcing her to take a step back.

"Would you mind holding him?" she asked one of the soldiers standing by who'd delivered the wounded men.

The man nodded uncomfortably, and took a position at the man's head, holding his shoulders down.

"Alright," Mercy said. "I'm going to proceed."

Sweat escaped her bonnet, rolling over her temple, along the front of her ear before following her jaw to her chin. Carefully, she reinserted her tool into the wound, feeling for the tell-tale scraping against the foreign object. The man winced and writhed, but his comrade was able to keep him down. Then she felt it, hard metal against soft flesh. Widening the jaws of her forceps, she slid them as far as the wound would allow around the object and bit down. The man panted heavily, and she could tell he was near to shock.

"I'm going to pull it out now," she said. "I need you to be strong. Take deep breaths, focus on that knot in the logs above you, it'll be over soon."

The soldier nodded uneasily.

Swallowing hard, Mercy began removing the shrapnel. It only took a few seconds, but it felt much longer. Her patient went rigid with the pain but refrained from fighting her. At last, the three-inch bit of iron was removed, and she wasted no time rinsing the wound with ale. Then she wrapped it with a fresh bandage.

Her patient breathed a sigh of relief as she tied the knot, his face red and wet with sweat.

"You did bravely," Mercy said. "The wound on your arm is smaller, it shouldn't be so bad."

After rinsing her tool in a bowl of water, she moved to the soldier's arm. She wanted air, the ordeal affected her more than she'd anticipated. Had she really been away so long?

"Alright," she said. "Let's get it over with."

The soldier nodded.

The wound on his upper arm was much smaller than the one in his leg, leaving her little room to maneuver the forceps. She prayed for mercy, that the bit of cannon burst had not penetrated deeply. The soldier went rigid as she probed the wound. Breathing a sigh of relief, she found it just under the surface. Pinching it with the instrument, she withdrew the small bit from his arm.

Her patient smiled with relief that the process had been a simple one. Again, Mercy cleansed the wound and wrapped it in a bandage.

"We'll need to change your dressings regularly, but I think you'll be alright," Mercy said as she tied the final knot.

"I was lucky," the soldier stammered. "Three of my mates . . ." His lips quivered. "They're dead."

"I'm so sorry," Mercy said, taking his hand. "You boys have suffered so much; the end can't be long now."

"They weren't even killed by the enemy," he said, shaking his head. "What kind of way to die is that?"

"They *were* killed by the enemy," Mercy said. "None of us would be here doing the things we're doing if it wasn't for the king, his tyranny, and his soldiers."

The man nodded.

"I'll check on you later," Mercy said, letting his hand go.

Looking up, she noticed Adelaide struggling with her patient and summoned her resolve. Moving in beside her, Mercy held the man's hands so Adelaide could work.

"Thank you," Adelaide huffed as she applied ointment to a large swath of burned flesh on the man's stomach.

The man winced and writhed, squeezing Mercy's hands so hard she thought he might crush them.

"Alright," Adelaide said when she'd finished with the ointment. "We need to sit him up so I can wrap it."

Mercy nodded. Looking intently into the soldier's eyes she said, "I need you to be strong. You're an American, we do what we have to, that's why the king can't beat us. When Adelaide says, we're going to sit up, it's going to hurt like fire, but that wound needs wrapping, because the Good Lord didn't spare your life so you could die of infection, do you understand?"

The soldier nodded his head.

"One, two, three!"

Together they got the man in a sitting position and Adelaide began wrapping a bandage around his torso. Mercy hooked her arms under his armpits and held on tightly. The boy winced and moaned but did his best to hold in the agony she knew he must be experiencing. In a few moments, Adelaide had finished, and he was able to lay back down.

"You conducted yourself bravely," Adelaide said. "I'm afraid we'll have to change your bandages once or twice a day for a few days, but it'll get better. I'll pray for you. Get some rest now."

The boy nodded and closed his eyes.

"Thanks for the help," Adelaide said.

"Somehow I'd forgotten what it was like," Mercy said.

"It's easier when you have friends to endure it with you," Adelaide said.

"Girls!" Mr. Musgrave hollered. "Don't just stand there, give me a hand!"

Adelaide squeezed Mercy's hand affectionately and they set off across the room to help him.

⁓

"Happy birthday," Adelaide said, taking a seat next to Mercy as they sipped coffee near the cauldron.

The rush of the morning had died down once their patients had all been tended to and were resting as best they could. The adrenaline had worn off and Mercy had found herself almost deliriously fatigued in its absence.

"Thank you," Mercy said. "Seventeen . . . the years have passed in a blink."

"They have," Adelaide agreed.

"When the war started, the soldiers were always much older than I. Now, many of them are my age, and they don't seem so old anymore. It seems like such a regrettably short life to lose."

"It is . . ."

The door of the hospital closed, and they saw Mr. Musgrave heading towards them, limping heavily on his pegleg.

"Looks like our rest is over," Adelaide said, gulping down the rest of her coffee.

Reaching the cauldron, Flint took a breath, looking at each of them with concern.

"What is it?" Mercy asked.

"I just got word, there was an assault on the fort at Savannah on the ninth of October. Our boys were decimated, including Count Casimir Pulaski who was leading a cavalry charge. They've called off the siege, we couldn't take Savannah."

"That's not a very nice birthday present," Mercy chuffed.

"There's more," Musgrave fidgeted. "It seems my predecessor was at the engagement rendering aid when he was struck by fragments of an exploding mortar round."

"What?!" Mercy gasped.

"I'm afraid the young Captain Davis has been wounded; the report didn't say more."

Mercy felt lost in shock as Adelaide wrapped an arm around her.

At a loss, Flint turned and limped back to the hospital, leaving the girls alone.

"What does he mean *wounded*?" Mercy asked. "Wounded how?!"

"The report didn't say," Adelaide said.

"What was he doing so close?"

"That's where you'd be," Adelaide said, squeezing her shoulders.

"But . . . that's different!" Mercy said.

"Mercy, he was right where he knew he was needed most, and you know that."

"He can't be wounded," Mercy gasped.

"Write to them," Adelaide suggested. "Request more information. Surely someone on his staff would relay your concerns and send word."

"What if . . ." Mercy started, looking into Adelaide's eyes, pleading.

"We don't know anything yet, Mercy. Wounded isn't dead. Write to them and pray."

"The ninth was a week ago . . ."

"Write, Mercy. It's all we can do. Your fretting isn't going to help any; I know it's hard, but you have to do what you can and leave the rest with the Lord."

Mercy stumbled her way back to the wagons, nearly bumping into Abigail as she stirred a stew near the fire.

"There's a letter on the buckboard for you," Abigail said cheerfully. "It's from Captain Davis."

Mercy clawed her way into the buckboard, ripping open the letter.

"My dearest friend, I hope this letter reaches you in time for your birthday. I'm sorry that I cannot be there to celebrate it with you. I'm sure you and your family are all sitting around the fire eating warm food and sharing gifts. I wish you every happiness on this special day and know that I too am celebrating the day of your birth. You seem to grow more lovely and radiant by the year and I expect I shall seem comely in comparison the next time we meet.

"The siege here has grown rather desperate, and it seems action must be taken. Pray for us, that we would have boldness to do whatever the service would require and find victory by God's merciful grace."

Mercy crumpled the letter in her hands as waves of emotion enveloped her; hanging her head, she sobbed.

"Good heavens, Mercy!" Abigail said in alarm, climbing up beside her. "What did he say?"

She couldn't speak, her heart couldn't find the words.

Abigail puller her into an embrace as Mercy continued to sob. Taking the letter, Abigail opened it and read it to herself. "Help me understand, Mercy. I see nothing here to be making any sort of fuss over."

"He . . . he's wounded, Mama," Mercy said.

"I didn't see that in the letter."

"Mr. Musgrave got a report. The siege failed, they tried to attack the fort and were crushed. Captain Davis was helping the wounded, and—and a mortar exploded."

"Good heavens," Abigail whispered. "How wounded?"

"Enough to make it into the report," Mercy said, catching her breath. "It didn't say anything more."

Deep inside, Mercy felt a pain like she'd never felt before, in a place in her heart she hadn't known she had. She knew too many wounds, she knew the odds, the grim hope, and the difficult lives many of those who did survive faced. She hadn't realized it before, but he was her knight, handsome, and bold, pure, and humble—infuriatingly humble—always right, and . . . and she loved him for it.

Chapter 18

Amputation?!" Mercy asked.

"That's what his letter says," Flint said. "His arm's been crippled; odds are an infection will take before long; it'll kill him if it isn't removed. His replacement says he's requested to be sent to Boston, to his father. Apparently, the captain says there is no one he trusts more to conduct the surgery."

It wasn't good, but he was alive. Mercy bit her lip to fight off the emotions welling up in her. Boston . . . his father hated him. Would he really treat him even though he thought he was a traitor? What if he handed him over to the redcoats?

"I need to go with him," Mercy blurted. "I have to see that he's looked after proper."

"They sent him by sea, lass, he'll be there any day now," Flint said.

"Then I have no time to lose."

Flint looked over at Adelaide, scratching his beard.

"You'd best let her go or she'll just run off in the middle of the night," Adelaide said.

"Fine," Musgrave sighed. "Look after the captain for us."

"Thank you," Mercy said, giving the crusty old man a hug.

"I'll write to you as soon as I arrive," Mercy said, giving Adelaide a peck on the cheek. "Thank you!"

Hanging up her apron, she dashed out of the hospital to find Abigail.

"You're back early," Abigail remarked as Mercy arrived at the wagons where the two mothers were teaching school.

"Mama," Mercy took a deep breath. "I need to go to Boston."

"Whatever for?" Abigail asked, stepping away from the class in progress.

"Captain Davis is alive; he was hit in the arm, and it needs to be amputated."

"Oh dear," Abigail said, putting her hands over her mouth.

"He's requested to be sent to his father in Boston. He says there isn't a better surgeon anywhere in the colonies. I have to go, Mama. I have to see him."

Abigail sighed, taking Mercy's hands. "We'll ask Henry about it tonight."

Mercy spent the remainder of the afternoon in knots, packing a bag, praying, and trying not to think about the fate of her friend.

The hours passed agonizingly slow, and eventually she found herself at the stables.

"Hey, guys," she said to a couple of chestnut geldings. "Tobias has been wounded. He told me once that when he had no one else . . . he'd always come talk to you."

Tears rolled down her cheeks as she fed them each half of an apple.

"I don't know if he'll be okay, or if he'll ever get the chance to thank you for being there for him, but I am. He's a good man, one of the best, and I feel so helpless right now. I miss him . . . you know?" She pressed her forehead against one of the horse's, stroking its neck.

She didn't know if it understood or not, but somehow, there in his presence, she didn't feel alone. She felt its peace and strength, the warmth of his life in each breath, the wisdom in his eyes. If the tables were turned, she was sure this was where he'd be.

"We'll get through this," she said. "God . . . help us."

When evening came, Henry had hardly finished saying grace when he brought up Captain Davis.

"Abigail tells me our good doctor has been wounded in the failed siege of Savannah, and that he's requested to be sent home to his father in Boston."

"That's right," Mercy said. "And I'd like to go to Boston to be with him."

There was an uncharacteristic quiet around the fire as everyone ate their dinner, waiting to hear Henry's response.

"That's a long way for a young woman to go alone. Benjamin and I are drilling every day, they're talking about sending us south in the spring," Henry said. "And who would look after you? Where would you stay, and for how long?"

"I don't know, Papa, but I'm pretty good at looking after myself. I could stay at the tavern in Cambridge in the evenings and make my way to Boston each morning."

"And what of his father, you said he was a Tory?"

"Not exactly a Tory, he doesn't like our cause, he supported the British with his practice while they were in Boston, but now he's just a doctor."

Henry frowned. "And how is his relationship with his son?"

"He's cut him off completely," Mercy sighed.

"I see," Henry said. "You know that most who receive amputation don't survive long after."

"That's why I have to go," Mercy pleaded. "I have to see to it he's looked after; I have to see him at least one more time."

"I could take her, sir," Jonathan offered, clearing his throat. "Make sure she arrives safely."

Henry thought about it for a moment. Mercy was shocked Mrs. Bell hadn't fired an objection to a young man and woman going alone, but perhaps they'd earned her good faith.

"When would you leave?" Henry asked.

"As soon as possible," Mercy answered.

"I could have us ready to leave by first light," Jonathan said.

Mercy could see a father's worry in his eyes as he glanced over at Abigail.

"You'll write us often?" Abigail asked.

"Yes, Mama. Every day if I'm able."

"Alright then," Henry sighed. "You have my blessing."

"Thank you," Mercy choked.

Everyone tried to be encouraging, tried to pass on strength and hope, and perhaps a little bit of joy, but the burden in her heart was too heavy. She finished packing before trying to sleep, but sleep wouldn't come. Infection was difficult to predict; in the time it took him to get to Boston, he may already be dead. On the other hand, if his body fought it, it may not spread much at all. Surely, he'd be taking every precaution, probably already tied it off.

She'd heard him refer to his father as the best before. His father's disappointment in him was the heaviest burden he carried, and the biggest sacrifice he'd made when joining the cause. She prayed his father would not be so indifferent as to refuse to care for him. If she had to, she'd conduct the surgery herself.

Outside, Theo hooted in a nearby tree. She wished she could bring him along, it'd be nice to have someone to talk to during the long, lonely hours of his recovery, but she doubted his father would allow an owl in his house, and Mrs. Hadley didn't care for him either. Truth be told, she had no idea if she'd be permitted in his house. What if she wasn't?

Around and around her worries and resolve chased each other in her mind, wearing out her heart, and putting her stomach in knots. Hour after hour she willed herself to fall asleep to no avail until in the soft greys of morning, she could hear the sound of horses being harnessed. Slipping out of bed, she grabbed her blankets and made up a bedroll, donned her dress, and stepped outside.

The October morning was cool and grey as a heavy autumn fog lay over the land. There was a bit of scuffling and Abigail appeared, carrying a knapsack.

"Here, there's a couple of firecakes and some biscuits in there. It'll get you part of the way, and here's a little silver to get you the rest of the way," she said, placing the coins in Mercy's hand. "You've grown up too quickly. I'm not ready to let you go yet."

"Oh, Mama," Mercy said, wrapping her in her arms. "I love you."

"I love you too . . . You be safe and get the good doctor well again."

"I will."

"We're all set," Jonathan said.

It was odd to see him out of his uniform and in plain clothes, but it was safer to travel as common folk than to advertise which side of the conflict you were on. Taking Mercy's hand, he helped her up into the buckboard of the flatbed. A final wave, and Jonathan snapped the reigns.

And she felt it again—the struggle—half of her heart already pining for home and family, and the other . . . the other longed for the open road and the adventures of the unknown. As the camp faded from view, she set her sights on that road, and the battles that lay ahead.

"Thank you for taking me," Mercy said. "I know you could've used the rest."

"The horses are the ones doing all the work," he said, giving the reigns another snap. "Besides, it's good to get away once in a while."

That seemed to be a theme with good men, always finding a humble way of downplaying their sacrifices. He didn't have to do it, didn't have to step in and save her, but he had. Oh, how her opinion of him had changed. People were incredibly surprising, once you got to know who they really were.

"How long do you think it'll take?" Mercy asked.

"Oh, about five-and-a-half days if we keep after it."

"It'll feel like a lifetime . . ."

"Not if you try to enjoy it a little. The fall colors are stunning once the fog lifts. You can't help him by fretting, Mercy, and I know he wouldn't want you to anyway."

"I know. . . . My imagination is a double-edged sword."

"He's going to need you to be strong and confident when he is not. Guys . . . we try to be invincible, which is good, until we're not. We can stand on our own, until we come up against that one thing we can't fix, can't seem to overcome, it's in that moment that it feels like everything starts to crumble. That's what it felt like when my father died."

"For me too . . ." Mercy said.

"Then you know what it's like to feel lost. He's always had two good arms, always been able to do things with his hands, be a doctor. Now, all that has changed. It isn't the loss of the arm, it's the loss of everything else that'll kill him. You'll have to help him find his way again if you're able."

"Like you are with Talise?" Mercy asked. "Don't think I haven't noticed you spend more of your free time in her camp than in ours."

He chuffed, turning a little red even in the soft morning light. "I swear, I was just trying to do you a favor by looking after her . . . but then, I don't know. I saw those kids needed someone, a father, and . . . and I liked being that man for them. They took me in, I didn't realize it, but they're rescuing me as much as I'm rescuing them. And Talise, she's borne all that she has so bravely, and still makes room for everyone else. She lives the life I dream of, not spending my days in a dusty ol' shop in Boston—a life of adventure. Living off the land, beholden to none—free."

"Have you mentioned your feelings to your mama?" Mercy asked.

"She's not daft," Jonathan sighed. "She knows where I've been. I think she's just waiting for me to tell her what I'm thinking, and I don't know how. Mama's changed a lot since the war started but presenting the notion of seeking Talise's hand . . . that may push her too far."

"And what does the Lord say?"

"I don't know . . ." he sighed. "I have so many other voices in my head, it's hard to make anything out."

"My mama's always telling me that's why the Lord chooses to live in our hearts rather than our heads . . . it's quieter."

"Yeah, but sometimes the heart doesn't make a lick of sense."

"Since when does faith make sense? David, a boy, running out to face a giant without any armor or a sword, Daniel in a lion's den, Noah building an ark when it hadn't ever rained, Rahab and the spies, Lazarus rising from the dead. . . . When did any of it ever make sense?"

"I guess most of the time faith seems a little foolish," Jonathan agreed.

"I think sometimes those voices in our heads that sound so confident and logical are really just cleverly disguised fear," Mercy said.

"Well, you seem to have it all figured out."

"Would you like me to talk to her for you?"

"Would you?!" Jonathan asked.

"What?! No! Of course not! That's your lion's den to conquer."

"See! You feel the same way I do about it!"

"I think your mama is . . . more understanding than she's ever been, and I wish you the best of luck."

Chapter 19

Mercy thought the five-and-a-half days on the road would have been ample time to get over her nerves, but now, as they entered Boston, her stomach churned with nauseating fury. Out in the harbor sat half-a-dozen ships at anchor, still others were being unloaded at the docks, and a couple more were sailing into the harbor, their white sails billowing in the midafternoon sun.

Jonathan called to folks they passed asking for the whereabouts of a doctor by the name of Davis. After a few tries, they were pointed to a larger house sitting up the hill a ways, looking out over the bay. Jonathan snapped the reigns, and the horses set off towards the house.

"It's a bit much," Jonathan said as they approached the large white structure.

It was two stories high with pillars in the front. Each floor was adorned with eight symmetrical windows flanked by black shutters. The house was quite stunning, a castle compared to the meager home Mercy'd lived in in Lexington.

"Would you like me to escort you?" Jonathan asked, setting the break.

"No," Mercy said, taking a deep breath. "This is *my* lion's den."

"Will you be alright? Should I wait for you?"

"No. I'll overcome, whatever it takes. Faith, right?" Mercy said, grabbing her bag and climbing down from the wagon.

Jonathan looked at her uneasily. "I'm going to check in on my father's shop, it's got a bedroom at the back. I think I'll spend the night there before returning in the morning. If you need me, I'll be there."

"Thank you, for everything," Mercy said, giving him a slight curtsy.

"Take care of yourself," Jonathan said, tipping his hat. "And him." With that he slapped the reigns, and the horses set off down the street.

Mercy turned to face the large oak door with its black cast-iron hinges and large black knocker.

"Lord, help me," she whispered, taking the cold metal knocker in her fingers.

Banging the knocker three times, she waited, listening for sounds of life inside. Bells on ships echoed from the harbor, seagulls squawked loudly overhead, searching the city for an easy meal, and then there as a clunk. The door opened and inside stood a tall man with a grey beard, cream-colored breeches, and an elegant black coat with brass buttons.

"Doctor Davis?" Mercy asked.

"No," replied the man. "I am his steward, Mr. Harding."

"Excuse me, sir. My name is Mercy Young and I'm here about Cap—I mean, Tobias Davis."

"He's only just arrived this morning, and in no condition to see any visitors," Mr. Harding answered.

"Just this morning? How is he, may I see him?" she asked.

"He's poorly, if you must know, and I told you, he'll be seeing no visitors."

"Please, sir, I'm no visitor, I'm one of his aides. I've been traveling more than five days, I need to see him, sir."

The old man studied her.

"I'm begging you, sir. I know about his arm, I'm here to see that he gets looked after proper."

"Wait here," the old man said, motioning for her to enter the house.

Mercy stepped inside a great room with an incredible curved staircase leading to the second floor. There were chairs for sitting, a piano, portraits adorning the walls in fancy golden frames. It was like no house Mercy had ever seen. She wandered along the wall studying the paintings, some were busts, others were of couples sitting together, another was a man on a horse, and another of a group of men clad in red, riding horses amongst a mess of dogs.

Approaching footfalls shook her from her wonderment and she found herself quite some distance from where the steward had left her.

"I hear you are an acquaintance of my son's," a second older man said as they approached.

"Yes, sir. I've known him since the night we met tending wounded on Dorchester Heights."

Captain Davis's father's mouth twisted into a grimace, and she knew she'd made a mistake.

"Do you see these portraits, Miss…?"

"Young, Mercy Young."

"Do you see these portraits, Miss Young?"

Mercy nodded.

"My family has faithfully served the crown for nearly twenty generations. That is, until my son turned his back on his people and became a traitor. A foolish upstart! A boy, who couldn't understand his duty! Who would help place cannons to rain iron down on his own father!"

"The cannons on Dorchester were never fired!" Mercy huffed. "And your son never turned his back on you! Only on a king and country who'd see us as lesser people than they themselves!"

"Ha! Lesser people!" the old man chuffed. "Maybe you, Miss Young, but my boy was kin to royalty! And he threw it away!"

"Then that makes him the nobler," Mercy said. "Do you intend to see to him? If not, I will take him."

"You?!" the old man scoffed. "And what would a camp wench know about his condition?"

"I know everything he taught me," Mercy answered coldly.

The two of them stood, jaws set, each staring the other down.

"I already have one traitor in my house, I don't have room for another," Captain Davis's father muttered.

Mr. Harding moved to usher her to the door, but she ducked his arm.

"Your son is the grandest and noblest man I know. He's never once spoken ill of you; in fact, he always spoke of you highly. In his eyes, you are the best. He wrote about you often in his journals; yes, I've read them, all he ever wanted was to make you proud. But his convictions looked beyond this mansion and your family's holdings, to the people who were suffering under the king's tyranny, and like Moses, he chose to serve with his people.

"I've watched him work himself to exhaustion, and beyond, putting everyone ahead of himself. His wound proves as much. He could've stayed back with the wagons, but his conscience wouldn't allow him."

She felt Mr. Harding grasp her arm, but she twisted it away, never breaking eye contact with Tobias's father.

"I'm not leaving until I've seen him," she said, clenching her jaw.

"Why?" asked the old man in a softer tone. "Why is he so important to you?"

"Because . . . because I . . ." She looked up at him. "I love him."

The words escaped her lips releasing a flood of emotions. Biting her lip, she frantically tried to hold back the storm, ready to fight Mr. Harding if she had to.

"And I'm not leaving until I've seen him," she said through grit teeth. She clenched her fists, her eyes brimming with tears.

"You certainly are the Mercy he wrote to me about," the old man said. "I had rather thought he was embellishing your character, but no, you appear to be every bit of it."

Mercy didn't reply as the man continued to look her over thoughtfully.

"I suppose I have no choice," he said at last. "Seeing this is a rebel port in which I am *graciously* allowed to continue to live on account I am the only doctor for some ways. Though I do believe that grace may be retracted if word got out that I'd spurned the infamous Mercy Young."

Mercy trembled as he held out his arm to direct her. Looking towards the hallway, she began by placing one foot in front of the other.

"My son is in the infirmary, at the back of the house."

Mercy walked slowly, keeping an eye on Mr. Harding. She wouldn't be at all surprised if the old man was just planning on throwing her out the back door, but she refused to go quietly.

As they walked, they passed elegant mahogany tables, chairs, tapestries and rugs, more paintings, doors, and then they entered a short hallway before arriving at a simple white door.

"This is where I keep my patients when they are in need of extended care."

He opened the door into a smaller room, and Mercy saw three tall cots, and on the middle cot laid a man under a white sheet, his bare chest and shoulders protruding out the top, his right arm, bandaged from his fingertips to midway up his forearm, lay beside him. His chest rose and fell peacefully with each breath.

She looked up at the doctor who nodded.

Stepping inside the room, she walked carefully to his side, her breaths catching in short gasps as she neared him. His face was pale, pocked with small burns, and unshaven; she lifted her wrist to his forehead and felt it. It was warm, not terribly, but he had a slight fever. He didn't stir when she felt him, and she wasn't surprised. His father had probably administered alcohol of some sort, and the trip couldn't have been very restful in his condition.

Next, she moved to his arm. She could sense his father's eyes following her. Sliding the bandage down a short way, she found what she feared. The skin was red and warm to the touch. His hand was also wrapped peculiarly, and from the looks of it, it was no longer complete. It didn't matter.

Turning from his arm, she ran the backs of her fingers lightly over his forehead and down his cheek. There was no denying it, in her heart she heard it clearly now, she loved him.

"Miss Young," the doctor said.

She wanted to stay, she wanted to be there when he awoke, be there to assure him that everything would be okay, she'd look after him. Let him know he wasn't alone in that big house with his bitter father and that rigid old Mr. Harding.

Taking one last look at him, she turned and walked to the door, unsure if she'd ever see him again. Once she was in the hallway, his father gently closed the door, and the three of them returned to the house.

"So, Miss Young, what is your prognosis?"

The question surprised her, was it a test?

"He has a slight fever, probably as a result of the infection in his arm, but given he's just traveled a fair distance in close quarters, it's possible it's the fever. Either way, in his compromised state it isn't a thing to take lightly. As for his arm, though I haven't seen the wound, it's clear by the warmth and smell it's already turned; there's no saving it."

"Your prognosis is correct. And how does this affect you?"

"A man is more than his arm, sir. It doesn't affect me in the slightest except in regard to my concern for his care. Will you save him?" she asked, looking up into his hazel eyes. "I can tend to him; anything you need, I can do it, I've been his assistant many years now."

"He's the enemy," the old man said, looking back down the hall. "He's a traitor and an embarrassment to his family, his name . . ."

Mercy wanted to argue when the old man continued.

"But . . . he is still . . . my son."

Mercy didn't know what came over her, but she crossed the two paces between them and threw her arms around him, burying her face in his chest.

"Thank you," she gasped.

For a moment the old man just stood there stunned, but then, very gently, she felt the weight of his arms wrap around her.

Chapter 20

To Mercy's surprise, the old man had given her a room in his house. She'd learned his name was Aldrich—Colonel Aldrich Davis, that is. He'd been a medical officer in the French and Indian War and was renowned for his medical knowledge.

They'd eaten quietly together that evening, neither of them saying a word, and then Mercy had gone to her room for the night.

In the morning, the doctor had found her sleeping in a chair, her head resting on the cot next to Tobias. He'd shaken her softly to awaken her for breakfast.

"I had a feeling you'd be there when Mr. Harding was unable to rouse you from your room this morning," he said as he set down his tea.

"Yes, sir," Mercy replied. "I didn't want him to wake and find himself alone."

"As I have no cases needing my attention this morning, I have decided to proceed with the removal of his damaged tissue after breakfast. You'd best eat light," he suggested. "I of course have my own assistants . . ."

"Oh, no, sir," Mercy said, looking up from her plate of eggs and bacon. "I'll assist you."

The old man looked at her, a little annoyed. "I've never worked with you Miss Young. All I have is your word that you are up to the task."

"My prognosis was correct, you said it yourself, and I *have* been assisting Captain Davis in every manner of grotesque procedure you can imagine. I am up to the task, sir."

"His life, that you hold so dear, depends on our miraculous precision, speed, and care."

"There's no one better, sir."

"Rather arrogant, aren't you?"

"No, sir. Just . . . confident. If he had his choice, he'd pick me."

Dr. Davis looked to his steward, who only shook his head. "You are a peculiar person," he said, studying her. "Very well, finish your eggs and we'll begin."

Mercy looked down at her plate. All of a sudden, she didn't feel very hungry. Looking up at Mr. Harding mournfully, she said, "I don't think I can."

The older man nodded, stepping forward and collecting her plate and utensils. "Godspeed, Miss Young."

"Thank you, sir," Mercy said, standing up from the table.

Setting off for the infirmary, Mercy was glad she hadn't finished her eggs. She was confident she was up to the task, but the conditions surrounding the procedure seemed to magnify the uneasiness she felt about the whole thing. Reaching the plain white door, she collected herself as best she could before pushing it open.

"Mercy?" Captain Davis whispered in surprise.

"I told you I had a special assistant," the doctor said. "She claims she rode over five days from whatever God-forsaken hole you rebels are hiding in to come and assist me."

Captain Davis looked away, trying to hide his arm. "I told Musgrave not to tell you."

"Whatever for?" Mercy asked, stepping up to the cot.

Tobias didn't answer.

"There's no place I'd rather be," Mercy said.

She watched a tear form at the corner of his eye, before it broke free, rolling past his ear and getting lost in his hair.

"Well, let's get on with it," Dr. Davis said. "It won't get any easier."

Mercy donned an apron hanging in the corner as the doctor laid out his tools on a small table. Then he brought over an odd contraption with leather straps and placed it near Tobias' arm. Next, he wrapped straps around the cot, tying down his patient's legs at the ankles and thighs.

Handing a bottle to Tobias, he said, "It's spiced rum, the sailors drink it. I picked up a taste for it during my time in the navy. You'd best take all you can stomach."

Tobias nodded, tipping back the bottle, his face white from fever.

"Fetch the flat iron over there and get it heating in the fire," Dr. Davis said.

Mercy nodded, fetching the iron by its wooden handle, placing the flat metal side in the fireplace to heat.

When Capt. Davis had drunk all he could, Mercy took the bottle and placed it back on the table. The doctor handed her a leather roll and she placed it in Tobias' mouth. For the first time since her arrival, she saw pity in the old man's eyes as he looked at his son. Then he picked up his son's arm and lashed it to the wooden brace.

Capt. Davis winced as the lashings were pulled tight on his lower arm. Two more were tied above the wound, holding his arm fast. Mercy noted the gashes in the wood from previous amputations. How many? She decided she'd rather not think about it.

"Alright, Miss Young," Dr. Davis said. "He'll likely pass out, but you must hold him still. If the cut isn't straight, or I have to start multiple times, he'll likely bleed to death. As soon as I finish, you must fetch me the iron to cauterize the wound and stop the bleeding, the sooner we burn it, the less blood he'll lose, and I've noted a reduction in odds of infection as well."

Mercy nodded, her stomach swimming now. Instinctively, she reached for his other hand and took it, holding it across his chest as she prepared to hold him down. Her hand felt the slightest squeeze and she quickly glanced at his face, but his eyes were closed.

"First, I'll use the knife to cut to the bone, then the saw. Again, we must be quick. Are you ready?"

Mercy nodded, tightening her grip.

"I hope your rebellion was worth it," the doctor said.

It'd been two hours since he'd passed out, and yet she could still hear the sound of burning flesh in her mind. Even though she'd vomited in the middle of it, she'd never let up, and Dr. Davis had praised her for her poise. The surgery had gone as well as such a thing can go, and Capt. Davis had conducted himself bravely until he'd blacked out, never once calling out.

Due to the infection, the doctor had been forced to remove most of his lower arm, leaving only a small nub below the elbow. Better to take too much than too little. All there was left to do now was pray.

At his desk, Dr. Davis's quill scribbled notes into a book while Mercy sat near the window sipping the tea Mr. Harding had brought her.

"He takes notes just like you," Mercy said. "After every procedure, every medicinal application, every loss. No matter how tired he is, he makes sure to record his findings while they're fresh."

The doctor stopped his scribbling, pondering her words. "For all his virtues, somehow he failed to add loyalty."

"Or perhaps he felt his duty and loyalty belonged to the people suffering under the king's rule, just like a good doctor is loyal to his suffering patients. It isn't the sick who tend to the sick but the well; the poor of the Americas needed those who were not, to stand for them, and your son did. He saw suffering, and he went to heal it. Even at great cost to himself. Isn't that what you taught him?"

The old man looked up at her, and she could read the conflict in his eyes.

"He supported the people even when the sickness looked unbeatable . . . he always does. And now, we just might win. He's more like you than you think. He's stubborn only for those he means to save, selfless to a fault, humble to the point of exhaustion, and loyal if he was the only man left standing. He's done you and your name proud, sir. Everyone who's known him would be proud to tell you so. You raised a good man, a man any father would be proud of, you raised the man that I have come to love."

"But we're subjects of the king . . ."

"A king can be wrong, sir. The Bible is filled with awful kings. What does it profit a man if he gains all this," Mercy swung her arms about the room, "but loses his soul?" As soon as the words escaped her lips, Mercy bit her tongue.

Like he'd been struck by a dagger, the old man slumped back in his chair, letting the quill fall from his fingers.

Lifting her cup, Mercy took another sip of tea, watching him out of the corner of her eye. She'd done it again, let her emotions and quick tongue get the best of her. Even Mr. Harding seemed to be at a loss as his eyes darted back and forth between them.

For a long while neither of them spoke; the room seemed locked under a dreadful silence, and her tea had run out. She felt foolish for being so brash towards him, a man who'd welcomed her into his home despite their differences, and she knew he must be a man of impeccable character to have raised such a fine son.

"I think I will go check on our patient," the doctor said at last.

His voice was tired and distant, and when Mercy rose to follow him, Mr. Harding subtly held up his hand signaling her to stay. When the doctor had disappeared down the hallway, Mr. Harding brought over a pot and poured her another cup of tea.

"He's a good man, Miss. I've served him most of my life, and I've never seen him turn a patient away, whether they could pay him for his services or not. I think deep down he is proud of his son, and he's worried, like any good father would be. He's been to war, and he didn't want his son to know the horrors of it the way he does. But I can assure you, he loves his boy, though he may have trouble communicating it."

"I didn't mean to offend him," Mercy said, taking her cup. "Sometimes my words get the best of me. It's a fault I continue to try and remedy, but it's apparent I still have a ways to go."

"I think it was an arrow well placed," the steward said. "Give him some time, he is not a man so proud that he cannot admit his own faults."

Mercy nodded.

"The procedure went well I trust?" Mr. Harding asked.

"Yes, sir. As well as can be expected. How a man can quiet his agony at a time like that I will never understand."

"Men have a knack for enduring pain quietly. But that doesn't mean they do not feel it deeply."

Mercy nodded.

"Do you require anything else, Miss?"

"No. Thank you."

Mr. Harding set off for the kitchen, leaving Mercy alone in the large empty room. She sipped her tea quietly under the watchful gaze of a dozen portraits, waiting for Dr. Davis to return with an update. The anxiety of the impending procedure was now replaced by the anxiety of his recovery.

Scanning the room, she noticed a folded piece of paper on the doctor's desk. The handwriting on it was familiar to her, a letter from Tobias. Standing up she inched closer to the desk little by little as though she were studying the paintings on the wall. Reaching the desk, she saw a small basket filled with letters from Capt. Davis. Each letter had a broken seal.

"Is this how you read my son's journals?"

The question caused her to jump.

"No, sir. He gave them to me," she said, turning to face him.

"I see," the doctor said, walking over to his desk.

"How is he?" Mercy asked.

"The burn was complete; I don't see any seepage. He's still asleep, and it would be best for him if he remains so for as long as possible. Before you retire for the evening, I'd like you to change his bandage and apply more ointment."

"Yes, sir . . ." Mercy answered. "Dr. Davis?"

The old man looked at her.

"Why didn't you ever write him back?"

He shook his head mournfully. "A fool's pride, girl. A fool's pride."

Chapter 21

December 21, 1779

It'll be Christmas soon. The army is once again encamped at Morristown to endure the long and cold winter months in the barrack cabins built two winters ago. Mama, David, and Mary-Beth have returned to Cambridge, Mama even brought Theo along. The snows have been heavy for so early in the season, and while it makes travel difficult, I do enjoy the beauty of the harbor dressed in its majesty.

Things here at the Davis mansion have been cold as well. Tobias's injuries have healed up well on the outside, and we are glad to be beyond the threat of infection. I know it will be a while before the wound is healed on the inside, he often winces with sporadic pains that come with a vengeance. It's the deeper wounds though, that worry me the most.

It seems with the loss of his arm, he has also lost himself as Jonathan predicted. He finds little value in his life as he fumbles with his left hand to do even the simplest of tasks like eating or writing. He treats me as little more than a nurse, and our conversations are short and one sided. He sees everything I do and say as a measure of pity rather than heartfelt affection; his indifference wounds, though I try to bear it graciously.

Dr. Davis, too, seems worried over his son's melancholy, and spends hours reading to him. Tobias rarely leaves his bed even though there's nothing to prevent him. It's though he really did die out there in that awful mortar blast, and what has come back to us is little more than a shell. Somehow, deep inside, I know my friend is still in there—lost in the storm, wounded, but alive.

I pray—I pray with all my soul—that God would enable me to be a light to guide him out of the darkness which has fallen over him. That he would see the grace and mercy of the Lord in sparing his life, and that there must be some grand purpose for the life he has left. The Lord knows my own heart has never been tested like it has these past months. It wouldn't surprise me in the least to look into the mirror and find grey hairs amongst the rest.

This terrible war has taken so much from all of us. I only have one wish this Christmas. Peace on earth and good will towards man. I appeal to heaven for mercy, but if that is not possible, then the courage, bravery, and endurance to achieve victory.

Mercy Young, 17 years old

"Would you mind if I brought him breakfast this morning?" Mercy asked the doctor.

"Suit yourself, but Mercy—"

"Yes, sir?"

"Guard your heart. He's not the man you once knew . . ."

"We'll see," Mercy replied confidently, taking the tray from Mr. Harding.

She carried the tray of bacon, eggs, toasted bread, and tea carefully up the stairs and down the hall to Tobias's room. Knocking once, she entered without waiting for a reply.

"Breakfast," she declared as she entered.

He was already sitting up in bed looking out his window towards the harbor. He didn't move, didn't even acknowledge her, just . . . kept staring.

Mercy set the tray down on the stand beside his bed. "It'll all be cold soon if you don't eat it now."

He didn't reply.

She reached up and gently touched his left hand. He jumped, scaring her half to death.

"What are you doing here?" he asked.

"I brought you breakfast," Mercy said, her hand resting on her pulsing heart.

Tobias looked at the tray. "I'm not hungry."

"You have to eat, everybody eats."

"Go home, Mercy. I can take care of myself."

"That's obvious," she replied, looking about the room.

He glared at her. "Why are you so stubborn?! I've never met anyone, man or beast, who could be so irritatingly stubborn in all my life! Go home! It's all gone, Mercy!"

"What's gone?!" she asked, stepping closer to him.

"Everything!" he said, reaching for the tray, but she caught his hand before he could send it flying across the room.

"What's gone, Tobias?!"

He reached to grab her hands holding his arm but there was nothing there to grab her with. He stared at his nub, still panting with rage, and then his eyes filled with tears.

"I am," he sighed, letting his nubbed arm fall. "I can't be a doctor anymore, Mercy. I can't help the cause, I can't even split firewood, or help build a stockade, or dig a hole, I can barely even feed myself . . . and I can't—" he drew in a trembling breath. "I can't take care of you."

She released his hand, and he let it fall to his lap.

"I had the foolish notion that after the war, somehow . . . maybe we could have continued together. That you would want to come with me, and we could have our own practice, and . . ." he shook his head. "Maybe a family? I wanted to give you the world, Mercy . . ."

The words hit her heart like rain on parched earth.

"Oh, Tobias," she said, taking a seat beside him. "You're still a really good doctor . . . and that is *not* a foolish dream."

"I have no hand, Mercy," he choked, holding up his nub.

Mercy gently wrapped her fingers around it, looking long into his eyes. "Then *I* will be your hands."

Tobias dropped his head into his hand, sobbing, and Mercy wrapped him in her arms, crying with him.

"You are *so* stubborn," Tobias choked.

"I know," Mercy agreed.

<hr />

She'd held him until he could allow himself a glimmer of hope again, and then left him to the Lord. Sitting alone in her room as the hours passed, she prayed. The enemy of his soul was far more cunning than the one who'd taken his hand. He'd come to believe the lie that along with his hand, he'd lost everything, including her . . . including himself.

The question now was, would he choose to believe God wasn't finished with him yet, or not? Up until now, he'd been living as though dead, but could it be that God had something bigger planned for him? It's easy to be confident in your faith when all goes well, when you feel in control; but faith is truly tested in the fire, and it's who you are *there* which reveals the true mettle of your faith.

Would he choose to believe? Would he choose to rise again in the midst of the fire and entrust himself to his faithful Creator? Or would he remain where he was—dead on the battlefield? She prayed earnestly he'd choose the former. Certainly, there was more to him than what the enemy could take in a single hand, but she couldn't believe it *for* him.

She didn't see him the rest of that day, and as she went to bed that night, her own faith was being tested. She'd never give up on him, not ever. She knew the man he was, she knew his character, and she prayed until her eyes closed in exhaustion that he would remember it too.

She awoke late the following morning and donned her dress. The house was quiet as it always was and, although she wanted to go to his room and check on him, she thought better of it, descending the elegant staircase to the lower level instead. She found the doctor sitting at his desk with a steaming cup of tea, reading over a letter.

"Ah, good morning, Mercy," he said. "Did you sleep well?"

"It was difficult on account of my thoughts, but I'm none the worse for wear."

"Go ahead and get some breakfast, I've already had mine."

"Thank you, sir."

She looked around expectantly for Mr. Harding, but he was nowhere to be seen.

As she took her seat at the table, she heard a door close at the top of the stairs and a set of footsteps clacking their way towards the staircase. Rising from the table, she stepped to where she could see the top of the steps.

Gasping, she saw him. Fresh from a bath, clean shaven, in fine linen breeches and a dress coat, his hair pulled back and tied neatly with a black bow. He smiled slightly when he saw her before descending the stairs, looking as dapper as ever he had.

When he reached the bottom, he held out his arm and she hooked it with her own and together they made their way into the great room.

"Good Lord in heaven," Dr. Davis said, lifting his eyes to the ceiling. "I never would have believed it."

"Father." Tobias bowed as the doctor rose from his desk to meet them.

"It's good to have you back," his father said. "You clean up nice, for a rebel." He smiled.

"All the praise belongs to Mercy, I'm afraid," Tobias said. "She helped me to see things as I ought."

"You're an extraordinary young lady," Dr. Davis said.

"I am beginning to believe stubbornness is my highest virtue," Mercy said, looking up at Tobias.

"You're both stubborn," the doctor said flatly. "You deserve each other."

Mercy smiled.

"I thought perhaps we could go for a walk along the harbor. Mercy's been telling me the fresh air would do me some good. Would you care to join us?" Tobias asked.

"Fresh air is precisely what I would prescribe, though walking through snow in the bitter cold is a young person's romantic notion and I'm afraid commonsense bids me stay indoors. You two go enjoy yourselves; I'll have Mr. Harding have warm tea awaiting you on your return."

The two of them donned their coats and opened the door.

"What's become of me?" Mercy heard Dr. Davis ask Mr. Harding behind them. "I've gone soft."

Outside, it took a moment for Mercy's eyes to adjust to the blinding white of their surroundings. A soft breeze swirled the few snowflakes that were falling from a pale-grey sky. Below them, ships in the harbor sat at anchor, their decks and masts blanketed in white, waiting in hibernation for the season to pass.

"Thank you, Mercy," Tobias said as they walked.

"For what?"

"For being the sun on my horizon and guiding me out of the night."

"It's what you asked me to be in your letter, remember?"

He nodded. "Had I known the burden I'd placed on you, I'd never have asked it so foolishly."

"Enough of that," she said, turning to him. "I would have been here all the same if you'd never said a word. This is where I belong. I once worried about you because you were a ship battling the storms with no harbor. I prayed one day you'd find yours . . . I just didn't realize at the time that the harbor I was praying for was me. I'm not going anywhere, Tobias, and I'm not sorry. You are no less a man to me than when you had both hands; those notions only exist in your own imaginations. Your storms are my storms, and we'll overcome them together."

Again, his eyes filled with tears, and he glanced away to hide them.

"No more tears," she reached up and brushed them away. "Today is a new day, you are who you are, and we are okay. Accept in your heart, that you *are* what I hoped for, you are more than enough, and I'm not here because I pity you. I'm here because I've finally realized this is where the Good Lord's been leading me, and for that, I feel entirely blessed."

He nodded.

"Our future is bright, so look to it."

He nodded again, and she turned, continuing their walk towards the harbor.

On the way, they passed a couple of young ladies walking along the shops who stopped in their tracks and watched the two of them pass. Tobias nodded politely, and Mercy smiled.

"Oooh, did you see the jealousy in those eyes?" she whispered, squeezing his arm. "We'll be the talk of the town by sundown."

Tobias scoffed. "How can you be so sure they weren't just admiring our appearance?"

"They're still staring," Mercy whispered. "And it's *your* appearance they were admiring."

Tobias shook his head.

"Just imagine if you were in your dress uniform." Mercy smiled. "They probably would have fainted."

Tobias scoffed, but she noticed he straightened his back just a little bit more, puffing out his chest.

Mercy walked along the wharf, drinking in the winter beauty and peace that, for the moment, was hers. But he, for his part, never stopped watching her. At first it made her feel silly, and she wanted to tell him to stop, but there was something else. In all the beauty, and all the snow, the thing that made it worth seeing . . . was her. And if that was what his heart longed for, then she'd let him.

She did all the silly things so he could see them. She stuck out her tongue and caught a snowflake, she twirled her dress, making the fresh flakes rise from the ground in a mystical cloud around her. She packed balls of snow together, making a miniature snowman on the top of a piling. Lastly, she picked up a ball of snow and threw it at him, laughing playfully.

To her surprise, a coy smile spread across his lips, and he stooped over to pick up his own ball. He packed it against his leg and hurled it at her with his left hand. It missed by several feet.

"It appears I'm at a disadvantage," he said.

"I'm sorry, Captain Davis," Mercy replied. "But I'm in no mind to take prisoners."

His eyes widened as she scooped up a handful of snow with each hand and raced towards him. He ducked the first ball, but she hit him squarely in the chest with the second. Stooping over, she scooped up two more handfuls as she closed the distance between them. This time her first ball hit him in the neck with some of it slipping beneath his collar, while the second flew over his head.

With no other option, and no room for retreat, Tobias charged his attacker as she stooped one last time to reload. Wrapping his arms around her, the two of them tumbled into the snowbank, laughing hilariously.

"You would be so cruel as to attack an unarmed man," Tobias jested, and Mercy burst out laughing.

Then she felt searing cold plunging down the back of her collar.

Screaming involuntarily, she fought to get away, accidentally landing a knee to Tobias's mid-section, doubling him over.

"Oh, my goodness!" she gasped, rolling him towards her. "Are you alright?"

"I'll be okay," he panted. "I surrender."

"Come on," Mercy laughed, pushing herself to her feet. She held out her hand and helped pull him to his feet, still gasping.

They were both soaking wet and beginning to shiver, but he smiled as he caught his wind.

"I think we'd best be getting back," he said, holding out his arm.

She took it, and they started back up the hill towards the house. Mercy could still feel the handful of snow he'd packed into her collar melting down her back as they walked. It was really good to have him back again.

Chapter 22

Thank you, but I don't think it'd be in the spirit of Christmas for a Loyalist, albeit a soft Loyalist, to celebrate and mingle with a host of rebels," Dr. Davis said.

"Rebels, Loyalists? I think that is precisely the spirit of Christmas, peace on earth and good will towards men. The only loyalty that matters at Christmas is that to our Savior, I don't think heaven is divided between Loyalists and Patriots," Mercy answered. "Besides, you can't spend it here all alone; *that* is opposed to the spirit of Christmas."

"I won't be alone . . . I'll have Mr. Harding."

"I've already invited Mr. Harding to the tavern party, and he's agreed to go," Mercy said, placing her hands on her hips.

The doctor eyed his steward.

"Forgive me, sir," Mr. Harding said. "The young lady is quite persuasive."

"She is that," Tobias agreed. "I've learned not to argue with her."

His father looked back and forth amongst the three of them, before rolling his eyes. "Oh alright, but just for a little while. I want to be home in time for a little reading in my chair before I'm off to bed."

"Thank you," Mercy said, stepping over to give him a hug.

"Alright, alright! I've already said yes."

Mercy smiled, letting him go.

"You keep this up and she's bound to be spoiled," the doctor said, looking at Tobias.

"She deserves to be," Tobias answered, holding out his arm for her to take.

"I will fetch your coat, sir," Mr. Harding said.

The snow had fallen deep and heavy, but Mercy didn't mind. Mr. Harding had harnessed the team to the sleigh and the three of them sat warmly under a heavy blanket. The team pulled them up the hill from the coastal town with little effort as the runners cut through the snow. Tobias made no attempt to release her arm the entire journey, and she felt no need to prompt him to do so.

As she swayed in the sleigh, Mercy pondered the rugged road which had brought her to this point. It hadn't been easy and began long before the day her papa had been captured on the green. So many circumstances, kings and Patriots, had brought them to that fateful night on Dorchester Heights. All the battles, narrow escapes, losses and victories, and here she was . . . sure, just like Abigail had said.

Mr. Harding pulled the sleigh up to the tavern where several others already waited, their horses chewing loudly on hay laid out for them at the hitching posts. Mercy's heart drummed with excited anticipation as Tobias hopped down and offered her his hand. She took it, dismounting gracefully to the ground beside him.

"Come, Father," Tobias said. "You'll see, these rebels are actually quite lovely."

Dr. Davis climbed down and the four of them entered the tavern.

"Bless my soul!" Abigail cried over the din, rushing to meet them at the door. Unabashedly she threw her arms around Tobias. "I've been worried sick about you, Captain Davis. It's the Good Lord's mercy we have you back again."

"Yes, ma'am." Tobias bowed. "This is my father, Dr. Aldrich Davis."

"It's a pleasure to have you, sir." Abigail said.

"The pleasure is mine," the doctor replied.

"I hope my Mercy hasn't been a burden," Abigail said.

"On the contrary, she's brought my son back to me."

"Mama," Mercy said, throwing her arms around her. "The tavern looks beautiful."

"Oh, that's all Mrs. Hadley's doing. I only helped a little."

"Aldrich! Aldrich, ol' boy, is that you?" a man called across the tavern.

"Charles!" Dr. Davis said in surprise, setting out across the room.

"One of his old friends from his time in the navy, I assume," Tobias said.

"Does it hurt?" Abigail asked.

"At times," Tobias answered. "I'm afraid my injury dictates that I will be needing Mercy to assist me . . . permanently."

"Permanently?" Abigail said with a coy smile. "Well, I'm afraid that is a matter you will have to take up with her papa, though he is not present here tonight."

"I intend to pursue the matter as soon as it is prudent," Tobias said, and Mercy felt her heart flutter.

"Mercy!" Mr. Hadley called out from behind the bar.

"We'd best go and give our greetings, or we'll be at it all night," Mercy said.

"See to it you find me later," Abigail said. "I sense we have some catching up to do."

"I will, Mama," Mercy said, giving her a peck on the cheek.

Together they made their way around the tavern catching up with friends and family amidst the merry celebration. They sang carols, ate plumb pudding, and drank cider. Older ladies gossiped while young ladies danced with eligible officers, and the old men talked of business, farming, and the high cost of goods.

Mercy danced with Tobias; his missing hand only meant they had to stand a little closer. She felt safe in his arms, loved, and enough. She was far from perfect, but he knew that, and still, he'd chosen her. She didn't feel a need to pretend she was anyone else, all they'd endured together had already revealed who she was. And she knew him, and his faults—especially the one where he was always right. Their friendship had always seemed special, and now she knew why.

"Where are your thoughts tonight, Miss Young?" Tobias asked as they danced. "I've seen that distant look in your eyes before."

"I'm here," she said, looking up at him. "I was just treasuring the road that brought me here and rejoicing in the Lord's faithfulness to have brought us to this place."

"Aye," he said. "I would have never made it on my own."

"Nor I," Mercy said. "I fear I would have chosen a lesser road and been the lessor for it."

"I meant what I said. I intend to talk to your father soon."

"I certainly hope so," Mercy scoffed. "It is the cruelest of men who'd play with a woman's heart."

"I wouldn't dare," he said. "Theo would probably gouge out my eyes."

Mercy snorted. "He really has been hard on you, hasn't he?"

"It's for the better," Tobias said. "It's prepared me to talk to your papa."

"Henry?" Mercy scoffed. "He's not scary."

"You've never been a papa before," Tobias said. "Henry would give his life to protect you or take a life if he had to."

"But he likes you," Mercy said.

"As a person . . . but as your husband? He'd be giving me his place in your life . . . that's not a thing any man would give up lightly."

Mercy hadn't thought about it like that. Henry loved her, from the moment they'd taken them in, he'd loved every one of them. Even when she made foolish mistakes, she never doubted her place in his heart, nor would she ever. Time had passed so fast, and now, now he'd be asked to let her go . . .

"That will be hard," Mercy agreed.

The dance ended and the two of them wandered over to the bar for some hot cider.

"My father seems to be getting along alright," Tobias said, taking a sip.

Mercy looked across the room to where the doctor was busy slapping his leg in merriment over memories with old friends.

"I can't remember the last time I heard him laugh," Tobias said.

"And in a room full of rebels, no less," Mercy added.

"People really can change," he said. "I never would have believed it."

"Maybe that's why it's so uncommon," Mercy replied. "Because we refuse to believe those who've made mistakes have it in themselves to overcome them."

"It isn't that, not for me anyway," Tobias countered. "I think the truth of it is, I didn't want to forgive him. If he changed, and I acknowledged it, I'd feel like I had to. He spent so much of his life making mine miserable, I didn't want to see him happy. But these past two months . . . he's been the father I never had."

"And have you forgiven him?" Mercy asked.

Tobias chuffed, but she saw the glimmer in his eyes. "I think I have."

She wrapped her arms around him. "Merry Christmas, Captain Davis."

"Merry Christmas, Mercy."

"One father down, one to go," Mercy said, letting him go. "I suppose it's entirely possible Henry could say no."

Tobias spat out his cider in a fine mist. "What?!" he choked, wiping his mouth with the back of his hand.

"I'm just agreeing with what you said earlier . . . he *could* say no."

"Why would you say that?" he said, looking at her wide eyed. "I never said he'd say no."

"Well, I just remember Abigail saying that a young man would likely have to fight Henry for me."

"Surely you understand she wasn't talking literally," Tobias said.

"Think what you like," Mercy said, taking another sip of her cider. "I'm sure you'll do fine."

"Why are you like this?" Tobias groaned.

"I had three brothers . . . it was every woman for herself," Mercy said matter of factly.

"Mind giving me a hand, captain?" Mr. Hadley grunted behind the bar as he struggled to lift another cider barrel.

"It's all that I have," Tobias said, slipping around the end to help.

Mercy smiled, he was beginning to accept what was and go with it.

Together they got the barrel situated and another song began. Captain Davis led Mercy out onto the floor to line up with the other couples. It was wonderful, enchanting even. A year ago, they'd gotten word about the attack on Savannah, and a short while later she'd gotten the news that he'd be leaving her. Now, they were together again, and perhaps this time, it was for all time.

As the music played and she twirled and bobbed, she remembered the first time he'd asked her to dance. The way he'd guided and protected her, making sure she was taking the correct steps. He'd done the same in the medical tent, always patient, always confident in her abilities, guiding, teaching, correcting, and praising. Even in the storm, when she'd gone after Jonathan, he'd come after her.

He was a lot like Henry, a lot like her papa. Perhaps that's why she felt so comfortable in his presence. His was a strength and gentleness she'd always known, like God was just handing her carefully from one good man to another, never leaving her on her own. Even though the circumstances were anything but gentle, He'd been there, ready to catch her, in every storm.

The last song finished, and everyone clapped for the musicians. The party had been one to remember and had lasted long into the wee hours of the morning. Mercy said her goodbyes, climbed into the sleigh, and the four of them set off for Boston by the light of a full moon.

"Tobias," Dr. Davis said as they rode. "I've decided to reinstate you as my heir. I believe I let my pride cloud my judgment, and perhaps I heaped on you a degradation of character to justify my own wounds, rather than being willing to see that we simply had two differing perspectives and therefore opinions on the war. I can't promise that I'll see everything the way you do, but I can see that you are a fine young man, a man this father is proud to call his son."

"And I'm proud to call you father," Tobias said.

Chapter 23

April 11, 1780

Tobias is making great progress, at least I think so. He is often short with himself as he works on his penmanship only to forget to lift his wrist and drag his cuff through the fresh ink. It is a difficult thing to write with his weak hand. He's learned to take care of himself for the most part, though he still cuts himself with the razor when shaving from time to time. He's able to buckle his buckles, button his buttons; I only help tie the bow to keep back his hair.

He's become terrible stubborn when it comes to his food, eating it like a savage rather than accepting my help to cut it properly with a fork and knife. He tries cutting on his own sometimes, but the meat so often slides on the plate with the motion of the knife that he wearies of it. On occasion he has tried to hold the fork in the crook of his elbow, and then cut with the knife; this is where he has found the most success. It will take time, but I am confident he will continue to progress and surprise us all, even himself.

The desperate war continues in the South, as we have received word that the British have laid siege to Charlestown, South Carolina. In the North we're kept on our toes by raids and skirmishes like that of flies in summer. While more annoying than anything, they do have an exhausting effect on our boys.

As Tobias has healed, his strength and resolve have returned. He intends to return to the South, only this time I will be going with him as his betrothed. I still can't believe Henry has given his blessing, though to keep me from the risk of widowhood he's asked that we wait until after the war to wed. A year ago, I'd have been in knots at the prospect of marriage, and now I find myself in knots at the prospect of waiting. My heart is a mystery even to myself.

Henry says General Washington is fixing to send General Gates to help in the South, and Henry and Benjamin will be marching out under him. Soon we will all find ourselves in a new war, in places we've never seen, and conditions we've never suffered. Abigail will follow us south with Mary-Beth, and David, while the Bells stay with Jonathan in the North. Adelaide is desperate to follow Ben, though Mrs. Bell has yet to give her blessing.

I look forward to the coming year with excitement and trepidation. To be so close and yet so far . . . nothing is certain. Perhaps with General Gates in the South, we will put the British on their heels. May God grant us the courage and wisdom to achieve victory and bring all of our loved ones home again.

Mercy Young, 17 years old

Glossary
of Uncommon or Difficult Words

Abysmal: Awful, dreadful, very bad

Annihilated: Totally destroyed, wiped out

Arrogant: Extraordinarily proud

Balm: A healing salve or cream

Brash: Recklessly confident, irreverently self-assertive

Brevity: Short, brief

Confidant: Someone with whom you share private or secret matters, a friend you can trust completely

Contaminated: Dirty, not pure, unclean, spoiled

Contempt: Believing a person is beneath consideration, unworthy

Correspondence: Communication, such as exchanging letters

Dapper: Handsome

Decimated: Destroyed entirely

Degradation: To bring something down, lessen value, to lessen the quality of something

Deliriously: To be slightly out of one's mind, confused or exhausted, unable to think straight

Dither: A state of agitation, flustered, worked up

Earnestly: With great desire

Embellishing: To add to something usually in a decorative way, like exaggerating a story, or adding jewelry to an outfit

Faltering: To stumble, trip, nearly fall

Finesse: With skill and tactfulness

Flank: The outside of something. In military use, the right or left flank is the right- and left-most troops in a particular formation.

Gargoyle: Hideous decorative sculptures adorning many old buildings in Europe

Garner: To collect or gather something

Gaunt: Sickly, skinny

Harbingers: Precursors, signs that something is coming

Heathen: Folks who don't believe in the Christian faith

Ignorance: Not knowing something, usually of no fault of your own

Inadvertently: Accidentally, unintentionally

Incredulously: Disbelief, unwilling to except that something is true, belief that something is being hidden

Inquiry: A question

Insist: Demand

Loathe: Deeply hate, despise

Lashings: Whippings, or straps used as tiedowns

Lobsterbacks: Slang term for British soldiers in their red uniforms with white straps

Mantle: Sleeveless cloak, like that worn by Elijah in the Bible that was passed on to Elisha. A symbol of handing down one's duty and position to another

Melancholy: A state of deep, thoughtful sadness

Mischievous: Trouble making, prone to be naughty

Nonsensical: Not making sense, illogical, thoughtless

Omnipresent: Present everywhere

Persuasion: Convincing, changing of the mind about something

Plight: Dangerous or difficult circumstance or situation

Prognosis: Estimation of the cause, outcome, and circumstances surrounding a disease or ailment

Prudent: Wise

Regaled: To entertain someone with talk

Relinquish: To let go of, retreat from

Reprisal: An act of retaliation

Ricocheted: Bounced off of

Salivate: To drool, produce saliva

Shrapnel: A bit of debris thrown from an explosion, usually metal, that causes harm

Slate: A dark gray metamorphic rock usually used for chalkboards

Sobered: No longer drunk or confused, thinking clearly

Sporadic: Random

Squaw: An Indian (Native American) wife

Stalemate: A situation where progress seems to be impossible

Strategic: Logical, intentional, militarily smart

Sweltering: Hot, humid, muggy

Terse: Curt, sharp, brief

Trepidation: Fearful anticipation

Tumultuous: Uproar, raging, disruptive, not calm

Uncannily: Unsettling, strange

Unrelenting: Won't stop, continuing without a break, oppressively continuous

It's not over yet!

I'd love to help other readers enjoy this book as much as you have. If you'd just take a minute and let them know your favorite scene, how the story impacted you, or what book or author you'd compare it to, it will help other readers find it. It's your best way to show your support for us and we greatly appreciate it!

Just scan this QR code to get to our Amazon Author page, click on the right book, and leave your review!

(Even if you purchased or received this copy from somewhere else, you're still eligible to leave a review on Amazon if you have an active account.)

Get your FREE Gifts from J. E. Ribbey!

FREE Story Quiz for A Mending Wound with a separate answer key!

FREE Printable Map of the Siege of Savannah!

To get these FREE resources and to find out what happens next to Mercy and her family, scan the QR code or visit our website at JERibbey.com!

Scan Me

About the Author

J.E. Ribbey, a husband & wife team, deploys a compelling writing style, combining a fast-paced action thriller with deep character immersion, giving readers an edge-of-your-seat adventure they will feel in the morning. A combat veteran, outdoorsman, and survival enthusiast, Joel enjoys mingling his unique experiences and expertise with his passion for homesteading and the self-sufficient lifestyle in his writing. A homeschooling mom, homesteader, and digital designer, Esther brings the technical, editorial, and design skills to the author team. Together with their four kids they manage a small farmstead in Minnesota, where, besides taking care of the animals and gardens, they also run an event venue and small campground. If you'd like to know more, you can find the Ribbeys on Instagram @j.e.ribbey or at their website JERibbey.com.

Made in the USA
Thornton, CO
01/24/25 08:45:36